Vermeer's Milkmaid

Manuel Rivas was born in A Coruña in 1957. He writes in the Galician language of north-west Spain. He is well known in Spain for his journalism and television programmes, as well as for his prize-winning short stories and novels, which include the internationally acclaimed *The Carpenter's Pencil*.

Jonathan Dunne is the translator of Manuel Rivas's *The Carpenter's Pencil*. His other translations from the Galician include the poetry of Rosalía de Castro and the short stories of Rafael Dieste.

Manuel Rivas

VERMEER'S MILKMAID

and other stories

TRANSLATED FROM THE GALICIAN BY
Jonathan Dunne

V
VINTAGE

Published by Vintage 2003

2 4 6 8 10 9 7 5 3 1

First published in Great Britain in 2002 by
The Harvill Press

Vintage
Random House, 20 Vauxhall Bridge Road,
London SW1V 2SA

Random House Australia (Pty) Limited
20 Alfred Street, Milsons Point, Sydney
New South Wales 2061, Australia

Random House New Zealand Limited
18 Poland Road, Glenfield,
Auckland 10, New Zealand

Random House (Pty) Limited
Endulini, 5A Jubilee Road, Parktown 2193,
South Africa

The Random House Group Limited Reg. No. 954009
www.randomhouse.co.uk

A CIP catalogue record for this book
is available from the British Library

ISBN 0 09 944707 X

Papers used by Random House are natural, recyclable
products made from wood grown in sustainable forests.
The manufacturing processes conform to the environ-
mental regulations of the country of origin

Printed and bound in Great Britain by
Bookmarque Ltd, Croydon, Surrey

TO YOYO, WHO DRAWS SHEDS FIT TO DREAM IN

Three of the stories in this book – "Butterfly's Tongue", "Saxophone in the Mist" and "Carmiña" – were made into José Luis Cuerda's highly praised film, *Butterfly's Tongue* (1999). These three stories were published separately by Harvill at that time (the translation of "Butterfly's Tongue" was previously carried out by Margaret Jull Costa).

The translator expresses his heartfelt thanks to the Tyrone Guthrie Centre in Ireland, where most of these stories were translated.

CONTENTS

WHAT DO YOU WANT
WITH ME, LOVE?

Love, I have come to you to complain
about my lady, who sends you
to where I sleep always to wake me up
and makes me suffer great pain.
If she does not want to see or talk to me,
what do you want with me, Love?
Fernando Esquio

I dream of the first cherry of summer. I give it to her and she puts it in her mouth, looks at me with warm, sinful eyes, as she possesses the flesh. Suddenly, she kisses me and gives it back to me with her tongue. And I'm hers for ever, the cherry stone rolling up and down the keyboard of my teeth all day long like a wild, musical note.

That night, "I've something for you, love."

I place the stone of the first cherry in her mouth.

But, in fact, she doesn't want to see or talk to me.

She kisses and consoles my mother and then leaves. Will you look at her, how I love the way she moves! She looks like she's permanently got her skates on.

Yesterday's dream, the one that brought a smile when the ambulance's siren cleared a way to nowhere, was that she was skating between plants and porcelain, in a glazed room, and ended up in my arms.

I had gone to see her first thing in the morning at the hyper-market. Her job was to keep the checkout girls stocked with change and to relay messages around the different sections. To find her, all I had to do was wait by the central checkout. And up she came, skating gracefully along the polished aisle. She did a half turn to brake, and her long, dark hair waved in time to the red, pleated skirt of her uniform.

"What are you doing here so early, Tino?"

"Nothing." I acted vague. "I've come for food for Perla."

She would always caress the dog. Needless to say, I had studied it all very carefully. Perla's night-time walk was rigorously timed to coincide with Lola's arrival. They were the most precious minutes of the day, the two of us in the hallway of the Tulipáns building, Flores district, caressing Perla. Sometimes she would fail to appear at 9.30, and I would prolong the dog's walk until Lola rose up out of the night, my heart tapping to the beat of her heels. On these occasions, I would get very nervous, and she was like a lady to me (where had she come from?) and I was a snotty-nosed boy. I would get very angry with myself. Looking back at me in the lift mirror was the portrait of a guy with no future, no job, no car, lounging on the sofa, digesting all the crap stuffed into the TV, scratching around the drawers for coins to buy tobacco. I had the sensation then that it was Perla holding the leash to take me for a walk. And if Mum asked why I had taken so long with the dog, she got a spiel delivered to her on the spot. That she might know better.

So I'd gone to the hypermarket to see her and draw strength. "The dog food is next to the babies' nappies."

She skated off, rhythmically swaying her long hair and skirt. It reminded me of the flight of those migratory birds, cranes or herons, that appear on documentaries after lunch. One day, for sure, she would come back and alight on me.

Everything was under control. Dombo was waiting for me in

the hypermarket car park with the car stolen that night. He showed me the weapon. I weighed it in my hand. It was an air pistol, but it looked impressive. It commanded respect. People would think I was Robocop or something. We had hesitated in the first instance between an imitation pistol and sawing off the hunting gun that had belonged to his father. "The sawn-off shotgun is more intimidating," Dombo had said. I had given the matter a great deal of thought. "Listen, Dombo, it's all got to be very calm, very clean. With the shotgun, we're going to look like a couple of space cadets, junkies or something. And people get very nervous, and when people are nervous, they do strange things. Everyone would rather professionals. The motto is each person does their job. No song and dance, no mess. Like professionals. So let's leave aside the shotgun. The pistol creates a better impression." Dombo was not too convinced about being barefaced either. I explained it to him. "They have to take us seriously, Dombo. Professionals don't make a fool of themselves with tights on their head." The confidence big old Dombo always showed in me was touching. His eyes shone whenever I spoke. If I had had the same confidence in myself that Dombo showed, the world would have bowed down at my feet.

We left the car in Agra de Orzán market and picked up the sports bags. At midday, just as we had calculated, Barcelona Street, pedestrianized and lined with shops, was full of people. Everything was going to be very simple. The door to the bank opened for an old woman and we followed her straight inside. I had rehearsed it all over. "Ladies and gentlemen, please do not be alarmed. This is a hold-up." I gestured calmly with the pistol and all the customers formed an orderly and silent group in the corner that I had indicated. A very helpful chap insisted on offering me his wallet, but I told him to keep it, we were not pickpockets. "You, please, fill the bags," I asked an employee with an efficient air about him. He did so in a flash and Dombo was infected by the

3

civilized climate in which all this was going on to the point that he thanked him. "Now, since we don't want any problems, please do not move for ten minutes. You've all been very kind." And so we went out, as if from a laundry.

"Stop, or I'll shoot!"

First of all, remain calm. I continue walking as if it had nothing to do with me. One, two, three more steps and off like a shot. Too many people. Dombodán doesn't think about it. He barges his way through like a rugby player. And there's me in a different film.

"Stop, you bastard, or I'll shoot!"

I take the pistol out of the open bag and turn around slowly, aiming with my right hand.

"What's wrong? Is there some problem?"

The guy who had offered me his wallet before. Standing with his feet apart and the revolver pointing straight at me, held in both hands. Now, that's a professional. A security guard in civilian clothes, I'll bet.

"Listen, boy, don't do anything stupid. Drop that toy."

There's me smiling, saying uh-uh. And I throw the bag in his face, all the money in the air, falling in slow motion. "Take that, you bastard!" And I break into a run, the people frightened, standing aside, what a disaster, the people standing aside, opening a cursed corridor in the street, a hole, a tunnel up ahead, a hole behind. It burns. Like a wasp sting.

The ambulance's siren. I smile. The male nurse looks at me confused because I'm smiling. Lola skates between miniature roses and azaleas, in a room with big windows. She comes towards me. Embraces me. This is our home. And she wants to give me the surprise, on skates, her pleated red skirt swaying in motion with her long hair, the cherry's kiss.

That night, through the glass in the door, I can read the Funeral Parlour's illuminated sign. "You are kindly requested to adopt a

4

moderate tone in the interests of everybody." Dombo, gigantic, loyal Dombo, was here. "Please condole my acceptances," he said to my mother with remorse. Now, don't tell me that's not funny. It sounds like a line from the Marx Brothers. It's enough to make you cry with laughter. He looked at me with tears in his eyes. "Dombo, you fool, get out of here, go and spend the money on a house with a room with big windows and a massive Triniton telly." But Dombo keeps on crying, with his hands in his pockets. He's going to soak everything. Tears like grapes.

Fa's here, Josefa, from the flat opposite. She for one always knew what the score was. Her look was an eternal reprimand. But I'm grateful to her. She never said a word. A good one, or a bad one. I would greet her, "Good morning, Fa," and she'd mutter something under her breath. Anything cooking in the world, she knows about it. But she wouldn't say a word. She'd help Mum, that was all. She'd smoke a Chesterfield with her at night and they'd drink a Lágrima from Oporto, while I played with the remote control. And now here she is, supporting Mum. She turns towards me from time to time, but she's stopped scolding me with her look. She crosses herself and prays. A professional.

Not long to go now. I can see the burial times on the illuminated sign. 12.30, in Feáns.

Lola says goodbye to Mum and heads for the door of the mortuary. The way she walks! Even with shoes on, she looks like she's flying. A heron or something. But what's this? She suddenly turns around, skates over in my direction with her pleated skirt and comes to land on the glass of the coffin. She looks at me in amazement, as if noticing me for the first time.

"Impressed, eh?"

"But, Tino, how could you?"

She has warm, sinful eyes, and her mouth is half-open.

I dream of the first cherry of summer.

5

BUTTERFLY'S TONGUE

To Chabela

"Hello, Sparrow. I'm hoping this year we'll finally get to see the butterfly's tongue."

The teacher had been waiting for some time for those in state education to send him a microscope. He talked to us children so much about how that apparatus made minute, invisible things bigger that we ended up really seeing them, as if his enthusiastic words had the effect of powerful lenses.

"The butterfly's tongue is a coiled tube like the spring of a clock. If a flower attracts the butterfly, it unrolls its tongue and begins to suck from the calyx. When you place a moist finger in a jar of sugar, can you not already feel the sweetness in your mouth, as if the tip of your finger belonged to your tongue? Well, the butterfly's tongue is no different."

After that, we were all envious of butterflies. How wonderful. To fly about the world, dressed up as if for a party, stopping off at flowers like taverns with barrels full of syrup.

I loved that teacher very much. To begin with, my parents couldn't believe it. I mean they couldn't understand why I loved my teacher. When I was only little, school represented a terrible threat. A word brandished in the air like a rod of willow.

"You'll see soon enough when you go to school!"

Two of my uncles, like many other young men, had emigrated to America to avoid being called up for the war in Morocco. Well,

I dreamt of going to America as well just to avoid being sent to school. In fact, there were stories of children who took to the hills in order to escape that punishment. They would turn up after two or three days, stiff with cold and speechless, like deserters from Barranco del Lobo.

I was almost six and everyone called me Sparrow. Other children of my age were already working. But my father was a tailor and had neither lands nor livestock. He would rather I were far away and not creating mischief in his small workshop. So it was that I spent a large part of the day running about the park, and it was Cordeiro, the collector of litter and dry leaves, who gave me the nickname. "You look like a sparrow."

I don't think I ever ran as much as in that summer before starting school. I ran like a madman and sometimes I would go for miles beyond the limits of the park, my eyes fixed on the summit of Mount Sinai, fondly imagining that some day I would sprout wings and reach as far as Buenos Aires. But I never got past that magical mountain.

"You'll see soon enough when you go to school!"

My father would recount as a torment, as if he were having his tonsils torn out by hand, the way in which the teacher would try to correct their pronunciation of the letters g and j. "Each morning, we had to repeat the following sentence: *Los pájaros de Guadalajara tienen la garganta llena de trigo.* We took many beatings for the sake of Juadalagara!" If what he really wanted was to frighten me, he succeeded. The night before, I couldn't sleep. Huddled up in bed, I listened to the wall clock in the sitting room with the anguish of a condemned man. The day arrived with the clarity of a butcher's apron. I wouldn't have been lying if I'd told my parents I was sick.

Fear, like a mouse, gnawed at my insides.

And I wet myself. I didn't wet myself in bed, but at school.

I remember it very well. So many years have gone by and still

8

I can feel a warm, shameful trickle running down my legs. I was seated at the desk at the back, half crouching in the hope that no one would realize that I existed, until I was able to leave and start flying about the park.

"You, young sir, stand up!"

Fate always lets you know when it's coming. I raised my eyes and saw with horror that the order was meant for me. That teacher, who was as ugly as a bug, was pointing at me with his ruler. It was a small ruler, made of wood, but it looked like the lance of Abd al-Krim.

"What is your name?"

"Sparrow."

All the children burst out laughing. I felt as if I were being whacked on the ears with tins.

"Sparrow?"

I couldn't remember anything. Not even my name. Everything I had been up until then had disappeared from my head. My parents were two hazy figures fading from my mind. I looked towards the large window, anxiously searching for the trees of the park.

It was then that I wet myself.

When the other children realized, their laughter increased, echoing like the crack of a whip.

I took to my heels. I began to run like a madman with wings. I ran and I ran the way you only run in dreams, when the Bogeyman's coming to get you. I was convinced that this was what the teacher was doing. Coming to get me. I could feel his breath and that of all the children on the back of my neck, like a pack of hounds on the trail of a fox. But when I got as far as the bandstand and looked back, I saw that no one had followed me and I was alone with my fear, drenched in sweat and pee. The bandstand was empty. No one seemed to notice me, but I had the sensation that the whole town was pretending, that dozens of censorious eyes

9

were peeping through the curtains, and that it would not take long for the rumours to reach my parents' ears. My legs decided for me. They walked towards the Sinai with a determination hitherto undetected. This time, I would arrive in Coruña and embark as a stowaway on one of those ships whose destination is Buenos Aires.

The sea was not visible from the summit of the Sinai, but another, even taller mountain, with rocks cut out like the towers of an inaccessible fort. Looking back on it, I feel a mixture of surprise and wistfulness at what I was capable of doing that day. On my own, at the summit, seated in a stone armchair, beneath the stars, while the members of the search party with their lamps moved about the valley below like glow-worms. My name crossed the night mounted on the back of the dogs' howling. I was not scared. It was as if I had gone beyond fear. So I did not cry, nor did I offer any resistance, when the robust shadow of Cordeiro came to my side. He wrapped me in his jacket and held me in his arms. "It's all right, Sparrow, everything's over."

I slept like a saint that night, lying close to my mother. No one had told me off. My father had remained in the kitchen, smoking in silence, his elbows on the oilcloth covering the table, the butts piled up in the scallop shell ashtray, just as had happened when my grandmother died.

I had the sensation that my mother had not let go of my hand all night. Still not letting go, as if handling a Moses basket, she took me back to school. And on this occasion, with a calm heart, I managed to get a look at the teacher for the first time. He had the face of a toad.

The toad was smiling. He pinched my cheek with affection. "I like that name, Sparrow." And that pinch wounded me like an after-dinner sweet. But the most incredible thing was when, surrounded by absolute silence, he led me by the hand to his table and sat me down in his chair. He remained standing, picked up a book and said,

"We have a new classmate today. This is a joy for all of us and we're going to welcome him with a round of applause." I thought that I was going to wet my trousers again, but all I felt was a moistness in my eyes. "Good, and now, let us begin with a poem. Whose turn is it? Romualdo? Come, Romualdo, come forward. Now, remember, slowly and in a loud voice."

Romualdo's shorts looked ridiculous on him. His legs were very long and dark, the knees criss-crossed with wounds.

A cold and dark afternoon . . .

"One moment, Romualdo, what is it you are going to read?"

"A poem, sir."

"And what is the title?"

"*Childhood Memory*. By Antonio Machado."

"Very good, Romualdo, carry on. Slowly and in a loud voice. Don't forget the punctuation."

The boy named Romualdo, whom I knew from carting sacks of pine cones like other children from Altamira, hawked like an old smoker of cut tobacco and read with an incredible, splendid voice, which seemed to have come straight out of the radio set of Manolo Suárez, the emigrant who had returned from Montevideo.

> *A cold and dark afternoon*
> *in winter. The schoolboys*
> *study. Monotony*
> *of rain behind the glass.*
>
> *This is the class. A poster*
> *shows Cain in flight,*
> *and Abel dead,*
> *next to a crimson stain . . .*

"Very good. What does 'monotony of rain' mean, Romualdo?" asked the teacher.

"That it never rains but it pours, Don Gregorio."

"Did you pray?" Mum asked, while ironing the clothes that my father had sewn during the day. The pot on the stove with the dinner gave off a bitter smell of turnip greens.

"We did," I said, not very sure. "Something to do with Cain and Abel."

"That's good," said Mum. "I don't know why they call that new teacher an atheist."

"What's an atheist?"

"Someone who says that God does not exist." Mum gestured with distaste and energetically ironed out the wrinkles in a pair of trousers.

"Is Dad an atheist?"

Mum put the iron down and stared at me.

"What makes you think your father's an atheist? How can you even think to ask such a stupid question?"

I had often heard my father blaspheming against God. All the men did it. When something was going badly, they would spit on the ground and take God's name in vain. They would say two things: "God damn it!" and "To hell with it!" It seemed to me that only women really believed in God.

"And the Devil? Does the Devil exist?"

"Of course!"

The boiling made the lid of the pot dance. From that mutant mouth emerged puffs of steam and gobs of foam and greens. A moth fluttered about the light bulb in the ceiling hanging from intertwined wires. Mum was moody, the way she always was when she had to iron. Her face would tense up when she was creasing the trouser legs. But she spoke now in a soft and slightly sad tone, as if she were referring to a waif.

"The Devil was an angel who turned bad."

The moth beat against the bulb, which swung from side to side, throwing the shadows into disarray.

"The teacher said today that the butterfly has a tongue, a very long, thin tongue that it carries around rolled up like the spring of a clock. He's going to show it to us with an apparatus they've to send him from Madrid. Isn't it amazing that the butterfly should have a tongue?"

"If he says so, it must be true. There are lots of things that seem amazing, but are true. Did you like school?"

"A lot. He doesn't hit us either. The teacher doesn't hit."

No, Don Gregorio the teacher did not hit. On the contrary, he almost always smiled with his toad's face. When there was a fight in the playground, he would call the children to him, "Anyone would think you were rams," and make them shake hands. Then he would sit them down at the same desk. This is how I made my best friend, Dombodán, who was big, kind and clumsy. There was another boy, Eladio, who had a mole on his cheek, which I would have smacked with great pleasure, but never did for fear that the teacher would have told me to shake his hand and moved me from next to Dombodán. The way Don Gregorio would show that he was really angry was by silence.

"If you won't be quiet, then I shall have to be quiet."

And he would walk towards the window with a distant look, his gaze fixed on the Sinai. It was a prolonged, unsettling silence that was as if he had deserted us in a strange country. I soon felt that the teacher's silence was the worst punishment imaginable. Because everything he touched was an engaging story. The story might begin with a piece of paper, having visited the Amazon and the systole and diastole of the heart. Everything fitted, made sense. Grass, sheep, wool, my cold. When the teacher turned to the map

13

of the world, we were as absorbed as if the screen at the Rex Cinema had lit up. We felt fear with the Indians when they heard the neighing of horses and the report of an arquebus for the first time. We rode on the back of the elephants that took Hannibal of Carthage across the snowy Alps, on his way to Rome. We fought with sticks and stones at Ponte Sampaio against Napoleon's troops. But it wasn't all wars. We made sickles and ploughshares in the smithies of O Incio. We wrote love songs in Provence and on the sea of Vigo. We built the Pórtico da Gloria. We planted the potatoes that had come from America. And to America we emigrated at the time of the potato blight.

"Potatoes came from America," I said to my mother at lunch, when she placed the dish in front of me.

"What do you mean, from America! There've always been potatoes," she pronounced.

"No. Before, people ate chestnuts. And maize came from America too." It was the first time that I had the clear impression that, thanks to the teacher, I knew important things about our world that they, my parents, did not know.

But the most fascinating moments at school were when the teacher talked about insects. Water spiders invented the submarine. Ants cultivated mushrooms and looked after cattle that produced milk with sugar. There was a bird in Australia that painted its nest in colours with a kind of oil it made using pigments from plants. I shall never forget. It was called the bowerbird. The male would put an orchid in the new nest to attract the female.

My interest was such that I became supplier of insects to Don Gregorio and he accepted me as his best pupil. There were Saturdays and holidays he would stop by my house and we would go off on an outing together. We would scan the banks of the river, heathland and woods, and climb up Mount Sinai. Each of these trips was like a journey of discovery for me. We always came back with a treasure.

A mantis. A dragonfly. A stag beetle. And a different butterfly each time, though I only remember the name of one that the teacher called an Iris, which shone beautifully when it alighted on the mud or manure.

On our return, we would sing along the paths like two old friends. On Mondays, at school, the teacher would say, "And now let us talk about Sparrow's bugs."

My parents considered the teacher's attentions an honour. On the days we went out, my mother would prepare a picnic for the two of us. "There's no need, madam, I've already eaten," Don Gregorio would insist. But afterwards he would say, "Thank you, madam, the picnic was exquisite."

"I'm quite sure he suffers hardships," my mother would say at night.

"Teachers don't earn what they should," my father would declare with heartfelt solemnity. "They are the lights of the Republic."

"The Republic, the Republic! We'll soon see where the Republic ends up!"

My father was a Republican. My mother was not. I mean that my mother went to Mass every day and the Republicans appeared as the enemies of the Church. They tried not to argue in front of me, but at times I overheard them.

"What have you got against Azaña? That's the priest putting ideas into your head."

"I go to Mass to pray," my mother said.

"You do, but the priest doesn't."

Once, when Don Gregorio came to pick me up to go looking for butterflies, my father said to him that, if he didn't mind, he'd like to take his measurements for a suit.

"A suit?"

"Don Gregorio, please do not take offence. I should like to repay you in some way. And the one thing I know how to do is make suits."

The teacher looked around in embarrassment.

"This is my trade," said my father with a smile.

"I have a great deal of respect for people's trades," said the teacher finally.

Don Gregorio wore that suit for a year and was wearing it on that day in July 1936 when he passed me in the park, on his way to the town hall.

"Hello, Sparrow. Maybe this year we'll get to see the butterfly's tongue at last."

Something strange was happening. Everyone seemed to be in a hurry, but they did not move. Those looking ahead turned around. Those looking to the right turned to the left. Cordeiro, the collector of litter and dry leaves, was seated on a bench, near the bandstand. I had never seen Cordeiro seated on a bench. He looked upwards, shielding his face with his hand. When Cordeiro looked like this and the birds went quiet, it meant that there was a storm on the way.

I heard the bang of a solitary motorbike. It was a guard with a flag tied to the back seat. He passed in front of the town hall and looked over at the men chatting uneasily in the porch. He shouted, "Long live Spain!" And accelerated away again, leaving a series of explosions in his wake.

Mothers started calling out for their children. At home, my grandmother seemed to have died again. My father piled up butts in the ashtray and my mother wept and did things that made no sense, such as turning on the tap and washing the clean dishes and putting the dirty ones away.

There was a knock at the door and my parents stared at the handle apprehensively. It was Amelia, the neighbour, who worked in the house of Suárez, the emigrant.

"Do you know what's happening? In Coruña, the military have declared a state of war. They're firing shots against the civilian government."

"Heaven help us!" my mother crossed herself.

"And here," continued Amelia in a low voice, as if the walls had ears, "apparently the mayor called the chief of police, but he said to say that he was sick."

The following day, I was not allowed on to the street. I watched at the window and all the passers-by looked like shrivelled up shadows to me, as if suddenly winter had fallen and the wind had swept the sparrows from the park like dry leaves.

Troops arrived from the capital and occupied the town hall. Mum went out to attend Mass and came back looking pale and saddened, as if she had grown old in half an hour.

"Terrible things are happening, Ramón," I heard her saying, between sobs, to my father. He had aged too. Worse still. He seemed to have lost his will. He had sunk into a chair and not moved. He was not talking. He did not want to eat.

"We have to burn the things that might compromise you, Ramón. The newspapers, books. Everything."

It was my mother who took the initiative during those days. One morning, she made my father dress up and took him with her to Mass. On their return, she said to me, "Come, Moncho, you've to come with us to the park." She brought me my best clothes and, as she helped me to do up my tie, she said to me in a very serious voice, "Remember this, Moncho. Daddy was not a Republican. Daddy was not friends with the mayor. Daddy did not say bad things about the priests. And most important of all, Moncho, Daddy did not give the teacher a suit."

"He did give him a suit."

"No, Moncho. He did not. Have you understood? He did not give him a suit."

"No, Mummy, he did not give him a suit."

There were a lot of people in the park, all in their Sunday best. Some groups had come down from the villages as well, women dressed in mourning, old countrymen in hats and waistcoats, children with a frightened air about them, preceded by men in blue shirts, with pistols strapped to their waist. Two lines of soldiers cleared a path from the steps of the town hall to some lorries with trailers fitted with awnings, like the ones used to transport the cattle to market. But in the park there was not the hustle and bustle of markets, but a grave silence, like that of Holy Week. People did not greet each other. They didn't even seem to recognize one another. All their attention was directed towards the front of the town hall.

A guard half opened the door and ran his eyes over the assembled throng. Then he opened it completely and gestured with his arm. From the dark mouth of the building, escorted by other guards, emerged the prisoners, their hands and their feet tied, roped in a silent line to each other. Some of their names I did not know, but I knew all their faces. The mayor, the trade unionists, the Athenaeum's librarian Resplandor Obreiro, Charlie, who sang with the Sun and Life Orchestra, the stonemason they called Hercules, Dombodán's father . . . And at the end of the line, hunched up and ugly as a toad, the teacher.

We heard some orders and isolated shouts that echoed around the park like bangers. There was a crescendo of murmurs coming from the crowd, that finally reiterated those insults.

"Traitors! Criminals! Reds!"

"Shout as well, Ramón, for the love of God, shout!" My mother held my father by the arm, as if she were using all her strength to stop him from fainting. "Let them see you shouting, Ramón, let them see you shouting!"

And then I heard my father whisper, "Traitors!" And then, as his voice grew stronger, "Criminals! Reds!" He let go of my mother's arm and drew nearer to the line of soldiers, his gaze fixed furiously on the teacher. "Murderer! Anarchist! Monster!"

Mum was trying now to hold him back and pulled on his jacket discreetly. But he was beside himself. "Bastard! Son of a bitch!" I'd never heard him aim those words at anyone, not even the referee at the football ground. "It's not his mother's fault, eh, Moncho? Remember that." But he was turning now towards me, urging me on with this mad look, his eyes brimming with tears and blood. "You shout as well, Monchiño, you shout as well!"

When the lorries drove off with the prisoners, I was one of the children who ran after them throwing stones. I desperately searched for the face of the teacher to call him a traitor and a criminal. But the convoy by now was a cloud of dust in the distance, as I stood in the park, with clenched fists, capable only of murmuring with rage, "Toad! Bowerbird! Iris!"

SAXOPHONE IN THE MIST

A man urgently needed money to pay for a ticket to America. This man was a friend of my father's and had a saxophone. My father was a carpenter and made country carts with oak wheels and the axle of alder wood. He'd whistle while he worked. Puff up his cheeks like a robin and make a lovely sound, the sound of a flute and violin, accompanied by the noble percussion of the tools on the wood. My father made a cart for a wealthy farmer, the nephew of a priest, and then lent the money to the friend who wanted to go to America. This friend had played some time before, when there was a working man's union and the union had a band. He gave the saxophone to my father on the day he sailed for America. And my father placed it gingerly in my hands, as if it were made of glass and would break.

"Perhaps one day you'll learn how to play *Francisco alegre, corazón mío.*"

This was a paso doble he liked very much.

I was fifteen and working as a labourer on the Customs site, in Coruña Harbour. My tool was a pitcher. The water from St Margaret's fountain was the one the men preferred and, as I made my way very slowly, I'd look in the windows of the shops and the Chocolate Express factory in Lugo Square. I'd go past a balcony with three cages full of brightly-coloured birds, and a blind man who was selling lottery tickets and flirting with the milkmaids. Sometimes

I'd have to wait at the fountain because there were other lads from other sites with other pitchers. We never spoke. On the way back to the site, I walked quickly. The workmen drank the water and I'd head out again for the fountain, looking in the window of the Chocolate Express factory and at the balcony with the three bird-cages, and stopping in front of the blind man who by now was flirting with the fishwives.

When I made the last trip of the day and put the pitcher down, I picked up the saxophone case.

For two hours in the evening I'd attend music lessons with Don Luís Braxe in St Andrew's Street. My teacher was a pianist who played in a variety club, and also earned a living with novices like me. We'd do an hour's singing and an hour with the instrument. On the first occasion he said to me, "Hold it like this, firmly and with affection, as if it were a girl." I don't know if he did this on purpose, but that was the most important lesson of my life. Music was like a woman waiting to fall in love. I closed my eyes and tried to imagine her, give her hair and eyes a certain colour, but I knew that for as long as all that came out of my saxophone was the brays of a donkey, that girl would never exist. In the daytime, as I made my way to and from St Margaret's fountain, I'd walk along with my pitcher, softly singing scales, lost to the world but for the women going by. Like the blind man with his lottery tickets.

I'd been attending music lessons with Don Luís for little more than a year when an extraordinary thing happened to me. I'd come out of class and stopped in front of the window of Faustino Shoes, over in the Cantón. I was standing there, holding my case, looking at these shoes like someone watching a Fred Astaire movie, when up came a bald, thickset man with an enormous forehead like the lintel of a door.

"What you got there, lad?" he asked without further ado.

"Who, me?"

22

"Yeah, you. Tell me that's not an instrument."

He was so tall and broad, he walked with his head held forward and his long arms hanging limply, as if he were tired of pulling the weight of the world.

"It's a saxophone."

"A sax? I knew it had to be a sax. Can you play?"

My mind went back to my teacher's patient gaze. "That's good, that's good." But there were times when Don Luís was unable to dissemble and the disquiet showed in his eyes as if I had indeed dropped a valuable glass piece on the ground.

"'Course you can," this strange man was saying, even though he had never heard me play. "Sure you can."

So it was that I joined The Blue Orchestra. The man's name was Macías, he was the drummer, and the boss to a degree. He needed a saxophonist for the weekend and there I was. My parents were in no doubt. When the bandwagon presents itself, you have to jump on it.

"Can you play *Francisco alegre*? You can? Right. Well, there you go."

He'd given me an address to attend the rehearsal. When I arrived, I knew there was no turning back. The room was on the first floor of the Chocolate Express factory. In fact, The Blue Orchestra had an enticing publicity agreement:

> *Chocolate Express,*
> *ah, it's the best!*

The band had to chorus this phrase three or four times during each performance and, in return, the factory gave each member a bar of chocolate. Just to make myself clear, this was back in 1949. These were times of insipid household aromas, thin soup, lethargy and black bread. Come home with a bar of chocolate and your little siblings' eyes would light up like candles before a saint. Chocolate Express was the best indeed.

> From beyond the seas,
> with dusk astern,
> it's the Orchestra Blue.
> The Blue Orchestra!

In truth, The Blue Orchestra had never left Coruña Bay, though it had once performed in Ponferrada. But that was the stylish mode of introduction at the time. America was a dream, for Galician orchestras as well. Legend had it that if you were given a contract to play in Montevideo and Buenos Aires, you could come back with a hat and the glossy sheen that goes with a full wallet. With my pitcher, it would take me a day and a night to travel the length of one of the avenues in Buenos Aires and the water would spawn frogs. That's what one of the workmen told me. Lots of orchestras had an American name. There was The Acapulco, from up in the mountains, which introduced itself like this:

> Tin-tin-tin, ti-ri-ti-tin . . .
> We address our distinguished audience in Spanish, having
> forgotten the Galician language on our last tour of South
> America.
> Peanuuuuuuuts!
> If you're looking to have it,
> buy yourself a packet
> of peanuuuuuuts . . .

Other orchestras wore mariachi costumes. Mexican taste has always gone down well in Galicia. In every song there was a horse, a revolver and a woman with a flower's name. What else does a man need to be the king?

The Blue Orchestra could put its hand to a Mexican ballad. But that was not all. The repertoire included boleros, cumbias, paso dobles, music hall, polkas, waltzes, Galician jotas, and more. A band that took itself seriously. Eight men on stage, dressed in black trousers and sky-blue shirts with white lacy frills and flounces on the sleeves.

Macías worked during the week in the Post Office. I imagined him stamping envelopes and pieces of paper as if he were beating the cymbals and bass drums. The vocalist was a chap named Juan María. He was a barber. A man with great flair. The girls were crazy about him.

"D'ya wanna dance, Juan María?"

"Take a hike, doll!"

And then there was Couto, who played the double bass and worked during the week in a foundry. Couto had a weak stomach, and had been told by his doctor only to eat porridge. He spent seven solid years on maize flour and milk. One day, during carnival, he arrived home and said to his wife, "I'll have myself a stew. Boiled ham, chorizo, the lot. And if that doesn't kill me, hunger will." He never had a problem after that.

The accordionist, Ramiro, repaired radios. A man with very sharp hearing. He'd come to rehearsal, perform a new piece and then say, "Here's one I plucked out of the air". He'd always say that, "One I plucked out of the air," and make a gesture with his hand, as if he were gathering in a handful of butterflies. Apart from his instrument, he played the reed pipe with his nose. A nasal waltz. A special number that impressed the audience, like the wise donkey of a circus act. But what I enjoyed was one of the mysterious songs he pulled from the air, the beginning of which I remember well.

> Rose dawn at the start of the day
> honeyed note shuddering on the violin
> the sleeplessness of fables which love lived in.

Then there was Comesaña on the trumpet, Paco on the trombone and my friend the tenor saxophone, Don Juan. An elderly, elegant man, who when we were introduced passed his hand over my head as if in a blessing.

I was grateful for that. In no time at all, it would be my debut. In Santa Marta de Lombás, Macías had told me.

"That's right, boy," Juan María agreed. "Santa Marta de Lombás, you'll go and you won't come back!"

II

It was Sunday, very early, when we caught the Lugo train. I wasn't so much nervous as in the clouds, as if I hadn't woken up yet and the train were a flying bed. Everybody treated me like a man, like a colleague, but I had the impression that I had shrunk overnight, that everything, from my top to my toe, including the trickle of my voice, had got smaller, while on the outside everything got bigger. Macías's hands, for example, were huge and heavy like a pair of weeding hoes. I looked at mine and what I saw were my little sister's hands wrapping up an ear of corn like a baby. God! Who was going to hold on to the saxophone? I sensed that perhaps the suit I had borrowed was to blame. It was too big for me and I slid around in it like a snail.

We alighted at Aranga Station. It was a summer's day and the sun was high in the sky. The representative of the Santa Marta de Lombás festival committee was waiting for us. He introduced himself as Boal. He was a robust type, with a glowering expression and a large moustache. He held on to two mules, which he loaded with the instruments and the trunk containing the costumes for the evening. One of the beasts turned round, frightened by the clatter of the drum kit. Boal squared up to it, his fist hovering before its eyes.

"I'll box your ears, Caroline! You know I will!"

We all watched Boal's fist. An enormous, hairy hammer swinging through the air. In the end, the animal bowed its head in submission.

We set off along a cool, cherry-scented path, alive with the chatter of birds, but soon took a dusty path across open heathland. There was now nothing between our heads and the sun's glare. Nothing, except for the birds of prey. My friends' early banter turned to a string of snorts, followed by subdued curses, which increased when their patent-leather shoes, covered in a film of dust, collided with the lumps of rock. Leading the way, robust and wearing a hat, Boal seemed to be pulling both men and mules.

Juan María was the first to cast a stone.

"Did you see that? A lizard, a massive lizard!"

In no time, everyone was hurling stones at the walls, rocks and lamp-posts, as if hundreds of lizards surrounded us. In front, Boal kept up a relentless pace. Occasionally he'd turn round towards the sweaty faces and say with an ironic smile, "Not far to go now!"

"I don't bloody believe this!"

When the horseflies started to sting, the curses went off like fireworks. The Blue Orchestra, roasting in the sun's flames, carried their ties and flicked them the way a beast flicks its tail to drive away the insects. By this stage, the trunk on the back of one of the mules resembled the coffin at a funeral. A kite hovered overhead, in the blazing sky.

Santa Marta de Lombás, you'll go and you won't come back!

As soon as the church tower came into view, The Blue Orchestra quickly smartened up. The men did up their ties, brushed down their suits, combed their hair, and cleaned and polished their shoes with a masterly wipe on their calves. I copied them in everything they did.

The sky-rockets were launched on our arrival.

"The orchestra's here!"

If there's one thing you enjoy the first time, it is the vanity of fame, however small and unfounded. The kids, whirling around us like butterflies. The women with a smile of geraniums in the window.

The old men peering out of the door like cuckoos in a clock.

"The orchestra! The orchestra's here!"

We waved like heroes raising the dead. I grew in size. My chest swelled with air. But suddenly I realized. We were really important. The centre of the universe. And I shrank like a snail. My legs turned to jelly. The saxophone case was so heavy I felt I'd stolen it from a beggar. I felt like a fraud.

We paused by the village cross and Macías placed his iron arm around my shoulder.

"Listen, lad, we each get taken off to the house where we're staying. Now don't you hold back. If you're hungry, ask for something to eat. And make sure the bed's a good one. That's the deal."

Then he addressed Boal sententiously, "I expect the lad to be well looked after."

"Don't you worry," the man replied, smiling for the first time. "He'll be staying at Boal's house. With me."

The ground floor was where the stalls were as well, separated from the kitchen by stone mangers, so that the first thing I saw were the cows' heads. They swallowed up the grass, licking it as if it were a cloud of sugar. The floor of the kitchen had been strewn with undergrowth. There was smoke from the hearth that made the eyes smart and the time uncertain. At the end of a very long table, a girl was sewing and did not leave off her task even when the man put the saxophone case down beside her.

"Hey you, coffee!"

She stood up and, without raising her eyes, went to fetch a pot from the sink. She then placed it on the trivet and, bending over and blowing gently, with the wisdom of an old woman, revived the fire. It was then, to my astonishment, that I noticed the floor moving at my feet. There were rabbits nibbling at the undergrowth, their ears stiff as eucalyptus leaves. The man must have understood my confusion.

"They make very good manure. And good roasts."

Boal took me, with pride, to see the livestock he owned. There were six cows, a yoke of oxen, a horse, the two mules that had carried our luggage, pigs and X number of chickens. That's how he said it: X number of chickens. The horse, he explained, could add up and take away. He asked it what two plus two were and it banged its hoof four times on the ground.

"You won't be going hungry here, boy. Hey you, bring the sponge cake. And the cheese. Hmm. Now don't tell me you don't want any. No one says no in Boal's home."

It was then, as she held the serving dish in her hand, that I was able to see her properly for the first time. She looked down, as if she were afraid of people. She was slight but her body was a woman's. She had her sleeves rolled up, revealing a washerwoman's sinewy arms. Her hair tied back in a plait. Almond eyes. I stretched out my hand to take something. What was happening to me? Heavens above! What are you doing here, little China girl? It was as if she'd never left me. The China girl from the school encyclopedia. I used to look at her, spellbound, while the teacher talked of the rivers named after a colour. Blue, Red, Yellow. Maybe China was just there, past Santa Marta de Lombás.

"She doesn't speak," Boal said in a loud voice. "But she can hear. That she can. Hey you, take the musician up to his room."

I followed her up the stairs to the top floor. She kept her head down, even when she opened the door to the room. In truth, there wasn't very much to see. A chair, a small table with a crucifix and a bed with a yellow bedspread. There was also a calendar from an ironmonger's with an image of the Sacred Heart.

"Fine, this is fine," I said. And I prodded the bed to show a bit of interest. The mattress was hard, made of corn-husks.

I turned round. She was standing against the light and I blinked. I think she was smiling. "Fine, fine," I said again, seeking her gaze. But she had her eyes fixed nowhere in particular again.

Dressed in their suits and ties, The Blue Orchestra assembled in front of the church. We were due to play the national anthem during High Mass, as the parish priest elevated the Host. I was so nervous I was changing size the whole time. Sweating in the squash of the choir stalls, I felt like a faint, insecure sparrow on a branch. The saxophone was enormous. I would not be able to hold it for much longer. And I was just subsiding when I noticed a saving breath in my ear. It was Macías, talking in a low voice.

"Don't blow, lad. Just pretend to play."

That's exactly what I did in the fairground, as people drank their vermouth prior to lunch. There was a small, warm-up dance. When I lost the note, I stopped blowing. But I made sure I kept up the swaying from side to side, the wave effect that Macías considered so important.

"It's gotta look nice," he would say.

The members of The Blue Orchestra were something else! I was convinced we'd be pelted with stones the first time I accompanied them on stage. They were so generous in their failings! And yet I was soon surprised by these men who earned next to nothing for playing at the ends of the earth. "Onwards and upwards!" Macías urged them on. And the swaying became more pronounced. And everyone became entwined in a rhythm that did not seem to come from the instruments but from the concerted life force of a few working men.

> *I have to see you, I have to see you, I have to see you,*
> *even though you hide and stay out of my sight.*

I tried to keep up with them, at least in the swaying. Every now and then, a soul seemed to flutter over me like a halo and I'd surprise myself with a good sound, but the orchestra's soul soon took to its heels like a robin frightened by a bray.

Lunch was with Boal and the little girl with the Chinese eyes. I definitely wouldn't be going hungry.

Boal sharpened the knife on his sleeve as a barber sharpens a razor on a strop and then, with a single slice, cut the suckling-pig on the dish in two. The brutal symmetry horrified me, especially when I found out that half of it, with its ear and eye, was for me.

"Thank you, but that's rather a lot."

"A man's a man and not a chicken," Boal pronounced, leaving no room for argument, as if he had summed up the history of the human race.

"What about her?" I asked, attempting some complicity.

"Who?" he said, genuinely shocked and looking around, holding the piglet's tail, until he spotted the girl, sitting in the light of the window above the sink. "Oh her! She's eaten. She's like a dicky bird."

For a few minutes he chewed voraciously, to dispel any last doubts as to what I should do with that pig.

"Let me show you something," he said suddenly, having wiped his mouth on that very useful sleeve. "Hey you, come here!"

The little girl reacted obediently. He grabbed her by the forearm in the snare of his hand. I was afraid she would snap like a bird's wing in a butcher's grasp.

"Turn around!" he said, as he rotated her and placed her with her back to me.

She was wearing a white blouse and a skirt with a pattern of red dahlias. Her long plait fell down to her buttocks, ending in a butterfly bow. Boal started to unbutton her blouse. I looked on in amazement, not understanding a thing, while the man fumbled with the buttons, which slipped in his coarse hands like pellets of mercury on the bark of a cork oak.

He finally unbuttoned the back of her blouse.

"Look, boy!" Boal exclaimed intriguingly.

I was spellbound by the butterfly bow and the plait pendulum.

31

"Look, boy, here!" he repeated, pointing with his forefinger to a pink flower on her skin.

Scars. There were at least six of those marks.

"Do you know what this is?" Boal asked.

I felt ashamed for her and for the cowardliness that gripped my throat. I wished I could have been one of those rabbits with pointed ears like eucalyptus leaves.

I shook my head.

"The wolf!" Boal exclaimed. "Did no one ever tell you about the wolf-girl? No? Well, here she is. The wolf-girl!"

What had been a strange and unpleasant situation suddenly entered the natural order of stories. I stood up and unreservedly went to take a closer look at the scars on her naked back.

"You can still see where she was bitten," Boal said, as if remembering for her.

"What happened?" I asked in the end.

"Go on, get dressed now!" he said to the girl. And with a gesture he invited me back to my seat. "She was four years old. I went to watch the flock and took her with me. It had been a hard winter. Good Lord! A terrible winter! And the wolves, well, they were hungry and swiped her from under my nose. From right under my nose!"

Apart from what the girl had been through, it was clear that Boal was personally very upset with the wolves.

"They laid a trap. We were in a meadow next to the woods. One of the swines came out into the open and made for the scrub. The dogs went crazy and chased after it. And I chased after the dogs. I left her there on her own, on a piece of sacking. I was only gone a couple of minutes. But when I came back, she'd disappeared. The wretches had swiped her from right under my nose!"

This man was in possession of a tale. All I could do was wait for him to unravel the end as soon as possible.

"No one understands what happened . . . She survived because it didn't want to kill her. That's the only explanation. The wolf that got her didn't want to kill her. All it did was bite her on the back. It could have bitten her on the neck and that would have been that, but no. Old people said the bites were to stop her crying, so she wouldn't give herself away. Well, she certainly paid attention. She turned dumb. Hasn't spoken since. We found her in a burrow. It was a miracle."

"And what's her name?"

"Who?"

"Your daughter?"

"She's not my daughter," Boal said very seriously. "She's my wife."

III

"She latches on to things. Goes into a trance. Something catches her eye and she won't let go."

I noticed the blood in my cheeks. I felt red as a beetroot. My elusive China girl wouldn't stop looking at me. I had come downstairs in readiness for the village dance and was wearing the frilly shirt.

"It's the outfit," Boal said with disdain. And then he turned to shout at her, "Silly little girl!"

Those eyes, with their pale green light, would follow me the whole night, fortunately for me, like two glow-worms. For I, too, latched on to them.

The dance was in the fairground, adorned from branch to branch of the oaks with a few paper garlands and nothing else. When it got dark, the only lights illuminating the dance were some lanterns hanging on either side of the stage and from the drinks stand. As for the rest, night had fallen with a tulle of mountain mist which shrouded the trees in petticoats and veils. In time, the mist grew thicker and blanketed everything in a ghostly substance, out of which only the happiest couples appeared, locked in an embrace,

33

twirling to the music, and soon swallowed up again by that sky that clung to the ground.

She, however, remained in view. Leaning against a trunk, her arms crossed, her shoulders wrapped in a woollen shawl, she wouldn't stop looking at me. From time to time, Boal would emerge from the mist like a shepherd anxious about his flock. He'd shoot a warning glance around, a mixture of cut-throat and poteen. But I didn't care.

I didn't care because I was fleeing by her side. We were riding the horse that could add up, over the hills of Santa Marta de Lombás, you'll go and you won't come back. Arriving in Coruña, at the Customs. My father was waiting for us with two tickets for the boat to America and, on the quay, all the workmen were cheering and one of them was offering us the pitcher to take a swig and giving the horse that could add up something to drink as well.

It was Macías, saying something in my ear, who made me open my eyes.

"You're doing brilliantly, lad! You're playing like a Negro, you're playing divine!"

I realized that I was playing without worrying whether I knew how to or not. All you had to do was let yourself go. My fingers moved of their own accord and the tightness had gone out of my chest, furnished by a singular pair of bellows. The saxophone was not heavy. It was light as a reed pipe. I knew there were people, lots of people, dancing and falling in love in the mist. I played for them. I couldn't see them. I could see only her, getting closer the whole time.

The China girl, fleeing by my side, while Boal howled in the night, as the mist cleared, on his knees in the fairground, holding the woollen shawl in his paws.

VERMEER'S MILKMAID

Of course, I'll never be able to repay what my mother did for me, nor will I ever have it in me to pen something similar to the *Correio* that Miguel Torga wrote in Coimbra, on the 3rd of September 1941.

> – "Son" . . .
> *And what follows*
> *Is so pure and so bright*
> *That even from my darkness it is visible.*

My mother was a milkmaid. She pulled a cart containing two large, zinc churns. The milk that she distributed came from the cows of my grandfather Manuel, in Corpo Santo, seven or eight miles from the city. This grandfather of mine, when he was a young man, one day held the parish priest's writing-pen in his hand and said, "What lovely handwriting I would have if I knew how to write!" Then he learned how to do so in a handwriting whose spirals, twists and turns resembled the tangles and flourishes of brambles and other vegetal forms. At the request of their families, he wrote hundreds of letters to emigrants. On his writing-desk, I saw for the first time, on a postcard, the Statue of Liberty, the Iguaçu Falls and a gaucho horseman on the pampas. We lived in the Monte Alto district of Coruña, on the ground floor of a house in Santo Tomás Street, which was so very close to the ground that there were cockroaches sheltering beneath the dislodged floor tiles. I sometimes played against them, volunteering them for the enemy army. I had discovered fear, but not terror. Let me tell you how I came into contact with terror. My milkmaid mother is pulling her cart with the zinc churns. I am playing with my sister María. Suddenly, we hear an explosion and an uproar in the street. We look out of the ground floor window to see what is happening. Our noses pressed against the glass, we discover terror. Terror is making its way towards us. My mother found us clinging to each other and crying in the bath. Terror was the carnival figure of the King.

It is 1960 and I am three years old. In the afternoons, I hear the prisoners singing hymns in the prison courtyard. At night, the flares of Hercules Tower turn like cosmic sails on the headboard. The lighthouse beacon is an important detail for me: my father is on the other side of the sea, in a place called La Guaira.

I am three. I remember it all very well. Better than what went on today, before I started this story. I even remember what the others maintain did not happen. For example. My godfather – and I don't know how he got it – brings a turkey for Christmas. On Christmas Eve, the animal escapes up the hill of Hercules Tower, pursued by all the neighbours. When they're just about to catch it, the turkey spreads its wings impossibly and flies out to sea like a wild goose. That was one of the things I saw that did not happen.

In 1992, I went to Amsterdam for the first time. This journey I had so longed to make was a kind of pilgrimage to me. I was dying to see The Potato Eaters. In front of this painting of mysterious fervour, the most deeply religious of all those I have seen, the true representation of the Holy Family, I suppressed the impulse to get down on my knees. I was afraid of drawing attention, like one of those eccentric tourists that wander about a cathedral in sunglasses and Bermuda shorts. There are two words in Spanish: hervor, boiling, and fervor, fervour. In Galician, there is only one: fervor. The glow from the boiling dish of potatoes ascends towards the faint lamp and lights up the faces of the peasant family, who contemplate the sacred food, the humble fruit of the earth, with fervour. I also went to the Rijksmuseum and there I came across Vermeer's *Milkmaid*.

The charm of the *Milkmaid*, painted in 1660, is in the light. Experts and critics have written very thought-provoking pieces on the nature of this luminosity, but the final conclusion is always a question mark. It is what they call Vermeer's mystery. Before finding its way to the Rijksmuseum, it had various owners. In 1798, it was sold by one Jan Jacob to a J. Spaan for the sum of 1,500 guilders. The inventory includes the following observation, "The light, entering through a window at the side, gives a miraculously natural impression".

In front of this painting, I am three. I know that woman. I know the answer to the enigma of the light.

> *Centuries ago, mother, in Delft — do you remember? —*
> *you were tipping up the jug in the house of Johannes*
> *Vermeer, the painter, husband of Catharina Bolnes,*
> *daughter of Mrs Maria Thins, that uptight lady,*
> *who had a son half deranged,*
> *Willem, if my memory does not fail me,*
> *who dishonoured poor Mary Gerrits,*
> *the maid who opens now the door*
> *for you, mother, to come in*
> *and go to the table in the corner*
> *and from the jug pour out butterflies of light*
> *which your family's cattle grazed*
> *in the green and sombre tapestries of Delft.*
> *Just as I dreamed it in the Rijksmuseum,*
> *Johannes Vermeer will whitewash with milk*
> *those walls, the brass, the basket, the bread,*
> *your arms,*
> *even though in the fiction of the painting*
> *the source of light is the window.*

> Vermeer's light, that enigma down the centuries,
> that ineffable clarity shaken from the hands of God,
> milk that you drew in the dark shed,
> at the bats' hour.

When I gave my mother the poem to read, she betrayed no emotion. This threw me. Though the poem talked about the light, perhaps it was too obscure. I went to a shelf and pulled down a book on Vermeer by John Michael Montias, which had a reproduction of the *Milkmaid*. This time, my mother seemed impressed. She stared at the print for a long time without speaking. Then she put the poem away and left.

After a few days, my mother came back to our house on a visit. She brought with her, as is her wont, eggs from her chickens, and potatoes, onions and lettuces from her vegetable garden. She always says, "Wherever you go, you should take something with you". Before leaving, she remarked, "I brought something for you too." She opened her handbag and produced a white piece of paper folded like a lace handkerchief. It contained a photograph. My mother explained that she had gone around all her sisters' houses to retrieve it.

The photograph was of her when she was single. Earlier than 1960, but much later, of course, than 1660. My mother does not remember who the photographer was. She does remember the house, the ill-natured lady, the half deranged son and the maid who opened the door. She was a very pretty girl, from the area around Culleredo. "One day, I went and a different girl answered. The other girl had been dismissed, but I never knew why." In the way she looked at me was a question, "And how did you find out about poor Mary?" Then she declared, "The scythe is always after the poor."

What my mother chose to ignore was the fact that the woman in the painting and in the photograph were as alike as two drops of milk.

HERE AND THERE

He had the sensation not of waking up, but of coming out of a torpor induced by warm lime tea. Ma was there, at the foot of the bed, goading him with those eyes of a dog sleepwalking.

"Where on earth can he have got to?"

"Keep calm, love."

They had waited for him until four in the morning, pacing up and down in front of the telephone, with an electric nerve running along the corridor to the lock of the front door.

"If only we'd called earlier!" she lamented. "Maybe he's at Ricky's. Or Mini's. Yes, I bet he's at Mini's. He told me her parents allow them to rehearse till late. Of course, they live in a maisonette."

"They may well do, but I doubt they let them kick up a fuss at night. Little angels, even if they played lullabies."

She folded her arms and searched for something to look at in the opaque wall of night.

"I wanted to talk to you about that, Pa. I think . . . I think we should try and make him feel more comfortable at home."

"More comfortable? What do you mean? He has the whole house to himself! The other day I turned up and there were four of them here, right here, in the sitting room, eating pizza and watching a video with guys and girls cutting off each other's legs and arms with an electric saw. Jesus! Why can't they watch porn films? I'd actually be pleased!"

"That's just the way they are. You have to understand them."

"Understand them? Do you know what I said to him? 'Hey, great film! What is it, the latest Walt Disney?' That's what I said to him. Pretty tough, eh?"

"He thought it was awful. He said you'd been a jerk, and you were always making fun of him in front of his friends."

"And what do you expect, hm? A clip round the ear. That's what I should do. Give him a good clip around the ear."

"Pa, please!"

"My father did, the day I told him to piss off. Piss off! I wasn't a kid any more. He gave me a slap that almost knocked me over. I'll be grateful to him for the rest of my life. It sorted out my ideas."

"Miro never told you to piss off."

"No. You're right. He told me to die. But he never told me to piss off . . ."

It was four in the morning, too late to call Ricky or Mini's parents. That would be like entering someone else's house uninvited, with mud on your shoes. He tried to convince her that it was better to go and sleep for a while.

"Everything's fine, you'll see. He'll be on his way back right now. Or he'll have stayed over at a friend's house. You need to rest, go on."

"No, you go to bed. You have to drive tomorrow. Do you want a lime tea?"

It was now seven and there she was, with bags under her eyes like the woman in charge of the cloakroom at a nightclub.

She was asking him silently to do something, before she was left alone and the corridor turned into a long tunnel.

"It's still a bit early. Keep calm. We'll wait for half an hour and then ring."

He dressed and shaved. He wet his head more than usual and combed back his hair, smoothing it down with his hands. He had a black coffee and felt the struggle in his head with the lime tea, the collision of a travelling salesman at full speed with a tramp who was walking by the side of the road. The salesman stood up and went towards the phone, followed by a woman waiting.

"I'm sorry to ring so early. It's Armando, Miro's father. I wondered, did he happen to stay with you last night?"

". . ."

"He didn't? Right. Sorry to have bothered you."

". . ."

"No, nothing's up. It was just . . ."

". . ."

"Yes, of course that's where he'll be. Thanks. And I am sorry.

"Nothing," he said. And he dialled the other number, Mini's parents' number. There was no answer and he dialled again.

"Nothing. It must be too early for them."

He took his wife by the shoulders and gave her a kiss. The whole of her seemed as light as the nightdress.

"You call in half an hour. I've got to go now. I'm already very late. Here, here, calm down. Come on, brighten up that face. Come on, a smile. Come on, darling, hey. That's better. We'll be in touch, OK?"

Before leaving, he peeped into his son's bedroom. On the pillow was a stuffed harlequin made of cloth with a porcelain head. There were days when this childish detail made him laugh, but today he gestured with distaste. The doll's expression seemed unnerving to him. A sad and doleful smile. On the wall, the biggest and most visible poster was of that guy, Steven Tyler, the lead singer of Aerosmith. He murmured, "Hey, how's it going, man?" His mouth was even bigger than Mick Jagger's. He had long, shaggy hair and a bare chest, with two fangs hanging from a necklace. Instead of trousers, he was wearing leopard-skin tights that hugged his packet unashamedly. In fact, he thought, the whole personality is in your face. For the first time, he was assailed by the suspicion that the poster was there because of him. They were the same age. Or were

41

they? Steven Tyler was older. When Miro told him, he had remained silent.

He stopped off at the warehouse and went over the merchandise. He filled the five suitcases. He left. He had gone some way when he received a warning. He was always guided by instinct. He had to take another suitcase of Superbreasts. He thought about phoning home from there, but changed his mind. If there were no news of Miro, he would only heighten the sense of alarm. He would end up spoiling the day and it was no joking matter. He thought about the competition. If the kid knew what life is . . .

He drove against the traffic. The cars heading in the other direction, towards the city, in a slow line, nodded their heads like impatient cattle. He stopped for petrol in Bens, before taking the motorway to Carballo. While the tank was being filled, he looked at the display of tapes for immediate consumption by motorists. A mix of the same old music, the covers discoloured by the sun. Mexican ballads by Javier Solís. Antonio Molina. Carlos Gardel. Chistes Verdes. Los Chunguitos. Fuxan Os Ventos. Ana Belén & Víctor Manuel. Julio Iglesias. Compostela Philharmonia. And there, in the middle, like a cursed coincidence contrived by a scriptwriter, a cover showing a cow with a tattoo on its haunch – Aerosmith – and a metal ring sticking through a teat. *Get A Grip*.

"I'll take this as well," he said, pointing to the tape.

Today, he would go all the way down the coast, at least as far as Ribeira. He had to time it well and stay just long enough in each shop. In Carballo, he stopped at Lucy's Corsetry. The owner of the shop was sifting through some garments and was slow to respond to his greeting. Be patient, he thought, the old dear's only just woken up and, besides, she's a bad temper.

"You're looking very well, madam."

"Don't try to soft-soap me at this hour."

"God helps those who help themselves."

42

"God? This is a disaster. A catastrophe."

"February's over. You'll soon see!"

"I don't want anything. Anything at all," she said, flatly refusing with her hands, as if she was inclined to throw him out.

"Now, you know I wouldn't let you down. Have I ever let you down? I tell you something will sell and it sells, doesn't it?"

"Yes, the pantyhose were going to sell in the winter. Do you know something? I've pantyhose here to warm half of Spain from the mouth downwards."

"I love it when you're angry. You look like, you look like . . . What's the name of that actress? Liz Taylor!"

"Yeah, yeah. I don't want anything."

"Let me show you one thing, just one. Can you imagine something better than Wonderbra, but at half the price? Now, I bet you can't."

"No. Go on."

"I wouldn't let you down. Take a look at this. The best bra in the business. It enhances the bust, but it's not a piece of armour. Touch it, touch it. Spring's on its way, Lucy, spring's on its way!"

He followed his route via Malpica. Then Ponteceso, Laxe, Baio, Vimianzo, Camariñas, Muxía, Cee, Corcubión, Fisterra. Things weren't going badly. He was glad he'd brought along extra Superbreasts! Thanks, gorgeous, sixth sense, you're always right. It must be almost time for lunch. He looked at his watch. Suddenly, he felt a slap, more painful than the slap his father had given him. Heavens! What was he thinking of? He ran, ran like a madman towards the telephone box.

"Ma? Is that you, Ma?"

" . . ."

"God, I'm sorry. I'm sorry, I'm sorry. I had real problems, Ma, believe me. Complications."

" . . ."

"Oh, nothing. A breakdown. And the boy? Has Miro turned up?"

". . ."

"He hasn't?"

". . ."

"Well, that's OK then. If he called, it means he's all right. What happened to him? Did something happen to him?"

". . ."

"Yes, I will talk to him. I'll have a very serious talk with him. Don't you worry. I'll make sure it doesn't happen again. Now, why don't you go and sleep for a while? Have a rest. I'll call you later. I've still got a lot of work to do. Have a rest, you hear?"

When he came out of the telephone box, on the quay in Fisterra, for the first time that day he noticed the sea. The March sun gave it a hard sheen, like that of steel. He went back to the box and dialled again.

"Ma? It's me. I'm sorry, eh? I'm sorry not to have called earlier. I don't know what came over me."

". . ."

"Everything'll be fine, you'll see. Everything will be fine. I love you, OK? Now, have a rest."

In the afternoon, at the beach in Corrubedo, there was a group of young people out surfing. He looked at them with envy. Not on his account, but on his son's. He wanted him to be like that, wearing those tight, brightly coloured suits. Contented, healthy, no doubt rich, in combat with the rude sea, sliding smoothly on the crest of the waves. Come on, he thought, he's not a bad lad. Apparently he even plays quite well, after a fashion. He'll be all right. I was.

He brought the day to a close in Ribeira. He was satisfied. In Next to the Skin, which stocked lingerie, he sold the last consignment of Superbreasts and of Basic Instinct knickers. His rival, the cocky salesman, who wore more rings than he had fingers, and that excessive tie like a bunch of gladioli, didn't half have a surprise in store for him when he arrived tomorrow. He'd outsmarted him, and he gives twice who gives quickly. He was satisfied and tired. When he shut the car boot, he felt that his eyelids would happily close as well. He decided to have a coffee and call from the bar.

"Hi, Ma. How are things?"

". . ."

"Good. Tell him to come to the phone."

". . ."

"How do you mean, don't say anything?"

". . ."

"Don't shout? You're worse than he is. A clip round the ear, that's what the boy needs."

". . ."

"He won't do it again? I should bloody hope not!"

". . ."

"Yeah, right. How nice of him! Where did he spend the night?"

". . ."

"Here and there, on his own?"

A silence fell between them, as if along the tunnel of the telephone could be heard the echo of the footsteps of a solitary insomniac walking and the tinkle of dripping water. He looked askance. All the customers in the bar were absorbed in the sports round-up on the television.

"How do you mean, here and there, on his own? Did he sleep in a doorway or something? He must have slept somewhere."

". . ."

"He didn't sleep?"

". . ."

"I'm not getting all uptight. What's he doing now?"

". . ."

"He was hungry, was he?"

". . ."

45

"That's good."

". . ."

"Ma, tell him, tell him . . . Bah! Don't tell him anything."

". . ."

"In Ribeira."

". . ."

"No, it's not raining."

". . ."

"I'm going to hang up. Don't worry about dinner. I'll grab something from the fridge."

". . ."

"'Night, Ma."

". . ."

"Yes, I'll drive slowly."

Before starting the car, he took a deep breath. The first neon lights turned on reluctantly and the light of the streetlamps was still weak. "Here and there, on his own," he murmured. Of all that had happened, that was what had most upset him. He heard Miro's footsteps along a tunnel. His face was painted white like a harlequin's. The image hurt him. He'd have felt much happier if he'd been out with his friends and watched the dawn smoking a lump of hash on the beach.

He put on the Aerosmith tape for the umpteenth time that day. Miro's present. Then, turning around to face Steven Tyler, his co-pilot, he gestured in complicity.

"You'd better drive."

His eyes were as heavy as the jaws of the car's infinite boot.

YOU'LL BOTH BE VERY HAPPY

Doctor Freire knelt down in reverential silence on the cushion of moss, as if the crag were an altar, and a holy stoup the fountain where the water formed a pool. On the way there, holding Fina's hand, he felt an ancient pleasure of oboe and harp that soothed the oppressive clock of his life as a specialist in heart transplants. But today the ritual had an added value.

"This is where it rises," he said in English, turning towards his guests.

His face beamed with pride, like that of the depositary of a biblical confidence. That piece of Genesis belonged to him. The water bubbled up in the sandy bed, between grass lint and glittering mica, and flowed through his man's veins before descending between alders. At this point, it was his heart that pumped the stream towards the Amoril valley.

Doctor Freire admired Doctor Kimball. In a way, the invitation was an expression of thanks. He had recently met him in person, at a medical conference that had brought them together in Santiago de Compostela. But for years he had been reading all his books, all his reports, and he was aware of his pioneering experiments in the replacement of living organs in transplants by synthetic equivalents. He had borrowed a large part of his medical knowledge from that man who worked on the other side of the ocean. Many of his doubts had been resolved at the computer terminal, thanks

47

to the information provided from far away by someone who today was sharing with him the stonechat's *vist trak-trak, vist*, that uneasy question that hangs in the dusk. Doctor Kimball was an authority in his field, a man of international reputation, and to Doctor Freire it seemed a miracle to have him there, leaning now, like him, over the stoup, with his eyes wide open, like a Buddhist monk interpreting the silent blinking of the bubbles.

When the American doctor and his wife, Ellen, graciously accepted the proposal to spend the weekend at their country house in the Amoril valley, before returning to Houston, Doctor Freire felt a mixture of surprise and gratification. When he told Fina the news, he could already feel the stimulating effect of the liquor of vanity, a reaction they savoured together as they made the preparations, and they did this unashamedly for each other, because it seemed to them that the occasion merited an open, gluttonous enjoyment, as a piece of good fortune that happens to come along. He was already imagining the effect on colleagues of opening a conversation with, "As Doctor Kimball said to me in my house in Amoril . . ." And she, Fina, though she had her feet more firmly on the ground, preoccupied as she was with her duties as a hostess, took the liberty of making a few select phone calls that she calculated would have the same impact as a society column in the newspaper El *Correo Gallego*.

So, there was the famous Doctor Kimball, seated now in front of the open hearth, with a glass two inches full of whisky, while Freire piled up the logs in a clever pyramid and lit the fire with the solemnity of someone performing a conjuring trick. On the other side of the room, Fina was searching for words in her stammering English with which to convey to Ellen that the painting they were looking at depicted the world as a carnival mask ("like a carnaval"), and that its author, Laxeiro, was the most sought after painter in the region.

It was she, Fina, who turned on the lights, as if induced by Ellen's observation before the painting,

"It's very beautiful . . . and also very strange."

Yes, Fina thought, it is a mysterious and dark carnival. In truth, she had never liked that painting. There was something unsettling and misshapen about it that bothered her. She would have preferred a more colourful and pleasing picture. A landscape like those they used to paint. Something really pretty, with everything in its place, where the fields were green, the roofs red and the sky blue. But this was a valuable picture. Everyone who understood painting told her so. And its value, according to those who knew about these things, would increase in the future, when the author was one of the dead people partying on the canvas.

The darkness also came from outside. The winter's night had suddenly fallen, and dressed the window-panes in mourning. When Fina turned on the lights, her husband turned around to protest from the hearth.

"No, love, wait a bit!

"The magic of an open hearth, as opposed to an enclosed fireplace, lies precisely in the trembling of the flames and shadows that the fire projects through the whole house. The sides of the hearth are open. It is like the cinema in three dimensions." Doctor Kimball followed the explanations with interest and smiled in agreement.

Fina took notice and moved with Ellen to where the newly lit fire began to crackle. Then, while the two doctors philosophized on fire and the human species, she remembered the dinner and made her way towards the kitchen. She did not like the dark. Her husband knew that she did not like the dark, but he had to be left today like a contented child showing another its toys. She looked out of the window in the corridor, but could see nothing. She opened the door and, in the light, sighed with the relief of someone escaping another's clutches. In the kitchen, with her sleeves rolled up and her cheeks coloured by the steam, Reme was rushed off her feet.

"Mm, that smells good!"

"I'm making you a proper stew, madam. The greens are fresh from the garden. They were still covered in hoar-frost!"

"Diego wanted to offer them a local dish."

"That's quite right. Nothing better than what's home-grown!"

Reme had been a lucky find. She was obliging and at the same time likeable and spontaneous. She and her husband looked after the house, keeping it clean and lived in, and seeing to any odd jobs that needed doing. She was a good cook, and her husband, Andrés, also called O'Courel, was a jack of all trades as well as a gardener; he might as easily repair a lock as lay new tiles where the damp had entered. He was, moreover, a very good conversationalist. He was not from Amoril. He had been born in the mountains and emigrated to Barcelona. He had, at times, left them speechless, when he embellished a story with Latin ditties or some surprising knowledge. For example, each fruit tree had its own fly. There was a different fly for the apple tree, peach tree, pear tree . . . And each animal had its own as well. The flies that hung around the cow were very different to those that flew about a donkey. On recalling this, Fina smiled, and Reme redoubled her efforts on seeing her satisfied.

"The clam sauce is ready as well, madam. The spring onion finely chopped and a touch of white pepper."

"I'm sure it will be lovely, Reme."

They were about fifty years old. They did not have children. When she talked about it, Reme grew sad.

"You two don't want to wait too long. For us now . . . You're still young. And you've the means to raise them. If I could, I'd have a dozen."

They were not talking about children now, but about the right time to serve up the dinner and make the best impression upon their guests.

There was a clap of thunder and the fluorescent strip light in the kitchen flickered and buzzed. But it stayed on. The two women looked at each other. Reme crossed herself.

"Goodness! There's quite a storm on the way."

Fina returned towards the sitting-room. This time, she went straight to the light switch and turned on the lights without worrying about her husband's reaction. But Doctor Freire made no remark. He said, "Listen, Fina. Skeletons in the cupboard." Then he translated the phrase literally into English. Doctor Kimball gestured that he had grasped the meaning immediately. Skeletons. Claps of thunder. They laughed.

Ellen related how, as a girl, she was not afraid of storms, unlike her brothers. Her parents had a holiday home on an island off the north of the east coast, near Canada, and sometimes the sky seemed to shatter like baubles in the hands of unruly children. At night, she would wake up and go and look out of the window. The flashes of lightning, she said, formed a fascinating spectacle. A festival of nature. But not any more, she confessed. The more the years went by, the more respect and fear she felt.

Doctor Kimball gazed at her ironically, "You can relax. I'll protect you always. I'll be your lightning conductor."

Their smiles froze in the shadows like cartoons in a comic strip. The lightning that fell cracked like a whip and shuddered on the roof of the house. There was a moment's silent commotion, until someone remarked that the electric light had gone out. Immediately, the voice of Reme was heard as she felt her way out of the kitchen, invoking the saints in heaven. The fire on the hearth finally guided her. When she reached them, her face was still flushed.

"It was terrible! The pans let off sparks before my eyes. The Devil's work!"

"It's all right, Reme, sit down for a while," Fina said.

"The fuses must have blown. My husband must be out there somewhere."

The thunder grew more distant and the water arrived. An excessive downpour that resounded in the gutters and beat with a hint of anger against the window-panes. The electric light did not come back on, nor was there any news of the long-awaited Andrés. That situation brought them closer to the fire, which was stoked up at the insistence of eyes and thoughts. Suddenly, Fina started from her seat and gazed in astonishment at the sitting-room window.

"Ah, there's Andrés!" said Reme in a calm voice.

"Gracious me, I was really quite afraid!" declared Fina in embarrassment.

She did not want to admit it, but for a moment she had thought that the hooded figure swaying an oil lamp was someone that the lightning had cast out of Laxeiro's painting.

"Good evening to you all!"

Andrés greeted them in a manly fashion and with feigned solemnity when they opened the door. He was heavily built, and his movements were so calm he seemed sluggish. He raised the lamp to his head and bowed slightly, in the old manner, in the direction of the guests. The makeshift hood, made by tying together the corners of a cloth sack, the thick eyebrows, the penetrating look, the bushy, ginger moustache, gave him the air of a hunter from the north. He took off his cloak, which was drenched, and asked permission to come into the room. He ceremoniously placed the lamp on the mantelpiece.

"Sure enough, the lamp's a relic! But you can see how useful it is in a spot of bother!"

"Andrés, what about the electricity?" Reme pressed him.

"Well, it looks serious."

"What do you mean, serious?" Doctor Freire enquired uneasily.

"Well . . . I'd say it's something to do with the line. Or the transformer. It's not the fuses. That's for certain."

"And how long will it take to repair?" Fina asked in an impatient tone.

"Ooh! With it raining like this . . ."

Andrés knew that he was the centre of attention, as if the return of the light depended on his words. He could reply "a few hours" or "a couple of days". Or both. He looked at Doctor Kimball. An amused imp made him say, "You never can tell with the Electricity Board. It could be a couple of days".

"You don't mean that!" Reme interjected, attempting to divert her husband from the path of libel.

"Last time it took them longer."

"Don't be so ridiculous!"

"I'm telling the truth. We're in the back of beyond here, if you'll forgive my saying so."

He turned to face his wife. One eye was pleading with him. The other looked daggers.

"They'll probably fix it tonight," he said with a smile, as if concluding a joke. "When it clears up a little, I'll head into town to see what's happening."

Everyone breathed a sigh of relief.

"Did you know? Andrés is a fortune-teller," said the host suddenly to the foreign couple. "Do you have your cards with you?"

"I always carry them in my pocket," replied the gardener, patting himself over the heart.

"Why don't you deal them for our guests," said Doctor Freire, pleased to be able to offer a really original spectacle.

"Not that, please!" exclaimed Reme.

"Why not? What's wrong with it?" the owner of the house insisted.

"No, nothing," she replied with resignation. "I'm going back to the kitchen now that the thunder has gone."

"Can he really foretell the future?" asked Doctor Kimball in an amused tone.

"He's incredible," said Freire. "He always gets it right. Come, Andrés. Please continue."

The gardener produced a pack of cards from his shirt pocket and settled down in front of the low sitting-room table. Doctor Freire was next to him. Opposite, the guests, Kimball and Ellen, were waiting to see what would happen. Fina stood smoking a cigarette, leaning against a column of the hearth.

"Right," said Andrés, in the solemn tone of someone beginning a ceremony. "This way of dealing the cards is called Seven in the Shape of a Cross. First, you cut them like this, seven times with your left hand. Then you place them like this, in the shape of a cross, face downwards."

Having dealt the cards, Andrés breathed in deeply and rubbed his hands slowly together, without raising his eyes. The only sound was that of the fire, which from time to time would produce a firework display of sparks. Finally, with a deliberate gesture like a priest's, Andrés turned over the card in the middle. A three of clubs upside down.

The diviner remained thoughtful for a moment. He glanced sideways at Doctor Freire. Then he gathered up the cards.

"Anything wrong?" asked the host.

"No. I'm going to deal them another way."

"He's going to deal them another way," said Doctor Freire to his guests with a smile. They nodded.

Without explaining anything this time, Andrés placed twelve cards in a circle and one in the centre.

He turned over the one in the middle. A three of clubs upside down.

Everyone reacted by laughing nervously. Doctor Kimball asked a question in English and his colleague translated it.

"Is it something bad, Andrés?"

"No, no. But I'm going to try another way."

"Ladies and gentlemen!" Doctor Freire proclaimed in a theatrical voice. "The third attempt!"

Andrés shuffled the cards repeatedly. This time he placed nine cards in rows of three, in the shape of a square. He turned over the central card, in the middle of the second row.

A three of clubs upside down.

The renewed, restrained laughter was close to being a gesture of alarm. They all looked at the fortune-teller and waited for an interpretation.

Andrés turned towards Doctor Freire and said in a low voice, with an outward show of normality, "I think we'd best carry on another day, sir."

"Why don't you pick up any more cards?"

"That card is a very bad sign. Believe me, we'd best leave it."

Doctor Freire looked at the couple and smiled.

"He says you'll both be very happy. He keeps getting the same result."

Doctor Kimball took Ellen's hand and asked his host to express their gratitude to the fortune-teller.

"Right, I'm going to see about the light," said Andrés, standing up. "The rain seems to have abated."

Fina followed him to the door. When he was already outside, she took him by the arm.

"What was wrong with the cards, Andrés?"

"Nothing, madam. Nothing."

"Was it something bad?"

"It was very bad, madam."

She felt upset. When the gardener was no more than a shadow in the night, Fina shouted after him.

"Was ours true?"

"What was that?"

"What you told us the other day."

"Yours was the honest truth, madam. You'll both be very happy. And soon you'll have a child.

"You'll have a child, sure enough. The child we'll never have," murmured the man in the darkness, treading hard on the muddy ground.

CARMIÑA

"So you've never been to Sarandón. I don't blame you. Why would you do that? It's a heathland which the wind cuts through like a razor."

O'Lis de Sésamo only ever came to the bar on a Sunday morning. He'd come in as the bells were ringing for eleven-o'clock Mass and his boots would be the first to leave their heavy imprint in the sawdust on the ground like the ink of a rubber stamp on a piece of paper. He'd ask for a sweet sherry, which I'd pour for him in a thin glass. He'd raise the glass, fixing me with his wild cat's eyes, and then withdraw to the window. In the background, the mass of Mount Xalo, like an imposing ox lying on its side.

"That's right, boy, the wind scrubbing like a hard brush.

"Heather, a few goats, scrawny chickens, and a house of rough stone with a half-naked fig tree. That's all there was in Sarandón.

"That's the house where Carmiña lived."

O'Lis de Sésamo took a swig the way priests do at the chalice, closing their eyes and all, hardly surprising, when they've God on their palate. He swilled the sherry around his mouth, and then clicked his tongue.

"Carmiña lived there with an aunt who never came out. A real mystery. People said she had a beard and things like that. But, to tell the truth, I never set eyes on her. I only had eyes for Carmiña, you understand. Carmiña! Did you know Carmiña when she was

57

young? No. How on earth would you have known Carmiña if you hadn't been born! She was a lovely girl, Carmiña, with plenty to hold on to. And she was game.

"Carmiña of Sarandón! To reach her, you had to drag your bum over the gorse, with a biting wind, sharp as a razor's edge."

There was now a war being waged in the sky above Mount Xalo. Fierce, dense, dark clouds snapped at the heels of others that were woolly and like sugar. From where I was standing, behind the bar, with my sleeves rolled up and my hands in the sink, it seemed to me that O'Lis's voice was growing hoarse and, against the light, he was acquiring the silhouette of a stoat or a marten.

"Another thing Sarandón had was a devil of a dog.

"Named Tarzan."

O'Lis de Sésamo spat into the sawdust and then trod on the clot like someone erasing a sin.

"God, I've never known such an evil dog! It wasn't just the odd day. It was always there. You should have seen it standing at our side, barking its head off, with hardly a let-up. But that wasn't the worst of it. The worst came when it stopped. You could feel, feel, the grinding wheels of hatred – like this – an irregular growl as it gritted its teeth. And then, the sheer resentment, the madness flashing in its eyes.

"No, it never left us.

"To start with, I pretended nothing was wrong. I even made as if to stroke it, but the little shit went even further off the rails. I'd go to Sarandón on a Saturday and Sunday evening. I couldn't get Carmiña to come down to town, to the dance. She said it was because of the old woman, who couldn't look after herself and had lost her reason, on one occasion even setting fire to the bed. I believed what she said, because Carmiña was not the shy type of girl. Tarzan would work himself up into a fury and she was game. She'd lead me by the hand to the shed, press against me with those

58

two lovely tits of hers and let me do and undo all I liked, with plenty of sighs.

"Carmiña of Sarandón! I was crazy about that woman. She was hot. She was randy. And always in a good mood. That mood of hers was quite something.

"'Devil of a dog,' I'd mutter when I couldn't take it any longer and felt the gnashing of teeth close behind me.

"It was a child's fear I had. And the little shit was able to sniff out my thoughts.

"'Go on now, Tarzan!' she'd say in a fit of giggles, but without pushing it away. 'Go on now, boy!' And then, with the dog panting like a corrupt pair of bellows, Carmiña would press harder against me, she'd ferment, and I would notice bells ringing out all over her body. To me, it was as if her heart were pealing inside the shed and, carried on the wind, everyone in the valley would be hearing those peals."

O'Lis de Sésamo placed the empty glass on the counter and signalled with his eyes for another sweet sherry. He took a swig, savoured it in the bowl of his mouth and then let it go like an air of nostalgia. "It's very good for you," he said with a wink. Soon the people would be coming out of Mass and the bar would fill with smoking Sunday voices. For a moment, as I put my hands back under the tap to wash the glasses, I was afraid O'Lis would let his story go cold. Fortunately, there was the mountain in the window, summoning his memories.

"I was very much in love, but the day came when I couldn't take any more. I said to her, 'Look, Carmiña, why don't you tie the dog up?' I sensed that she wasn't listening, as if she were in another world. She was always sighing. You know who did hear though. That fucking dog. It suddenly left off barking and I thought at last we'd be able to romp about in peace.

"Pah!

59

"There I was on top of her, on some trusses of grass. Before I realized what was happening, I felt an icy tickling and it was as if my whole body had ceased to function and lost its pulse. It was then that I became aware of the creature's moist stump, its muzzle snuffling around my private parts.

"I jumped up and let out a curse. Then I grabbed a stake and hurled it at the dog, which took to its heels, whimpering. But what annoyed me most was when she ran out after it, looking like she'd just woken up from a nightmare, 'Tarzan, here Tarzan!' When she came back, alone and with a heavy heart, I was smoking a cigarette, sitting on the log used for cutting firewood. I don't know why, but I began to feel strong and robust as never before. I went over to her and held her, ready to consume her with my kisses.

"I swear it was like fondling a limp sack of flour. She wouldn't respond.

"When I left, Carmiña was standing up on the hill-side, still and silent, almost lost, her body lashed by the wind. I don't know whether she was looking in my direction."

O'Lis de Sésamo's ears had turned red. His eyes shone with the green light of a wild cat, set in a face of harrowed earth. My hands burned under the coldwater tap.

"That night," O'Lis continued, "I went back to Sarandón. I was carrying a goading-rod, for driving cattle. The moon bobbed among the storm clouds and the wind droned in fury. There was the dog, at the gate in the stone wall. There was a hint of suspicion in the way it growled. Then it let out a weak bark, warily, until I placed the rod level with its mouth. It was then that it opened wide to bite the rod and I thrust it in like a sword. I thrust it all the way down. I felt the point tearing its throat and piercing the softness of its insides.

"Ah, Carmiña! Carmiña of Sarandón!"

O'Lis de Sésamo spat on to the ground. Then he took the last swig and held it against his palate. He let out a sigh and exclaimed, "Tastes bloody nice, that!"

He put his hand in his pocket. Placed the money on the counter. And gave me a pat on the shoulder. He always left before the first customers arrived straight from Mass.

"See you next Sunday, boy!"

His boots left their mark in the sawdust. The imprints of a solitary animal.

THE GAFFER AND IRON MAIDEN

To Arsenio Iglesias and Basilio Losada

The boy cursed, got up in a foul mood and kicked the stool over. The white-haired man, while addressing him, looked at his T-shirt, with the words Iron Maiden on it, and a monstrous spectre holding on to the ends of a high-tension cable, with flashing eyes. The spectre's hair was snow-white and very long.

"What are you doing? Put the stool back!"

They were watching the match on TV. The opponents had drawn level and it was looking less and less likely that Deportivo da Coruña would win the championship. There were only five minutes to go before the game ended. At the far end of the kitchen, the mother was making lace. The industrious sound belonged to the natural order of the house. You only noticed it when it was gone.

"It's his fault," said the boy resentfully.

"Whose?" The white-haired man was feeling fed up as well.

"Whose do you think? The man's an oaf!"

"Why are you calling him an oaf? You don't even know what you're talking about!"

"We were winning, we were winning and he goes and swaps a forward for a defender. He's always on the defensive. Can't you see that he's always on the defensive?"

"Is he on the pitch? Tell me. Is he on the pitch? Are there not eleven players out there? Why do you always blame him?"

"Because it's his fault! Why doesn't he bring on Claudio, I'd

63

like to know? Why not? We were winning and he goes and swaps Salinas. Makes a mess of everything!"

"Aren't you always saying that Salinas is useless?"

"He is, but why swap him for a defender?"

"The others are playing as well. Don't you realize that the other team's playing as well? We were dying of hunger. Do you remember when we were dying of hunger? We were sunk and now we're second. What the hell more do you want?"

"Don't start ranting at me! You're as bad as each other," the boy said, making a spiral in the air with his finger. "First one thing, then another. Watch out, take care. Football's like this, it's a complicated game. One rant after the other."

"You'll miss him. You mark my words. You'll miss him soon enough!"

The commentator announced that the time was up. The referee looked at his watch. Then the home bench appeared on the screen and the camera focussed on the gaffer's distressed face. The white-haired man had the strange sensation that he was in front of a mirror. He buried his head in his hands and the coach copied him.

"Take early retirement!"

The white-haired man looked at the boy as if he had shot him from behind. The mother stopped what she was doing and this had the same effect as a soundtrack in a suspense film.

"Why do you say that?"

The boy was conscious that he was on the verge of crossing a line of barbed wire. His tongue grazed against the trigger like a finger that has taken to it and no longer obeys the head's orders.

"I'm saying he's old. He should go!"

They had argued a lot all the way through the league, but without getting angry. Now, at last, the matter was settled. The white-haired man lapsed into silence, mesmerized by a point on the screen. The camera searched for the referee, who brought the whistle to his mouth and blew three times for the end of the match.

"Well, that's just fucking brilliant, isn't it?"

"Don't talk like that in the house!" the mother scolded. When she took her tired eyes off the lace-pillow, she had the impression that she was viewing the world through a lattice-window.

"I'll talk how I damn well like!" The boy marched off, slamming the door, which made the night blink.

The boy was now steering the boat and the father scanned the sea. The other barnacle fishermen hung off Roncudo de Corme, the cliff on Death Coast. It was almost the last hour of low tide. From this moment, until an hour into high tide, each minute was sacred. This was the time when it was possible to set foot on Penas Cercadas, the feared shoals where the waves of the Outer Sea broke. Only the well-versed fishermen venture here, the ones who can read the lines of foam, the writing on the rocks. Like a cormorant or a seagull, you must measure the sea's whimsical clock.

The sea has many eyes.

Every time they approached Cercadas, the boy recalled this phrase that his father had solemnly repeated on their first outing, like someone handing down a password for survival. There was one other fundamental lesson.

The sea only wants the brave.

But today his father was silent. He had not spoken to him even when he woke him up. He knocked with his fist on the door. Drank his coffee at a gulp, with a bitter gesture, as if it contained salt.

His father had another rule that he always observed before jumping on to Cercadas. For at least five minutes, he would study the rocks and follow the flight of the sea birds. A custom that, to start with, when everything seemed calm, the boy thought made no sense, but that he learned to respect the day he discovered what a large wave really was. Absolute silence. His father shouting out to him from the rock to steer the boat away. And suddenly, out of nowhere, the din of a hellish machine, of a giant digger. In a state of shock, trembling, with the boat flooded by the intake of water, he anxiously searches the silhouette of Penas Cercadas. There, upright, with his legs bent like a gladiator's, holding the barnacle lever like a spear to pierce the heart of the sea, is his father.

As many eyes as the sea. Today, the father's look is vague. He is about to say something. He chews over the words like gum. Listen, you know. Yesterday, I didn't. But the father suddenly takes the fork and net, stands up, turns his back on him and prepares to jump. He only has time to manoeuvre the boat round for him. He keeps the engine running slowly, with an oar propped against the rock to protect the boat. He waits for instructions. A gesture. A look. It is he who shouts, "Be careful!"

The sea is calm. The boy is hung-over. He drank and returned home late in the hope that the night would clean out the day's events, in the same way that the liver cleans out cheap liquor.

He wet his hands in the sea and moistened his eyelids, rubbing them with the tips of his fingers. When he opened his eyes, he had the impression that years had gone by. The sea had darkened and acquired the muddy colour of a cheap, local wine. He looked up at the sky. There were no clouds. But it was the contracted silence that alerted him.

He searched for his father. Incomprehensibly, he had his back to the sea. He shouted, making a trumpet with his hands. He shouted with all his might, as if blowing through a seashell on the Day of Judgement. Concentrating on his father's movements, he completely forgot to steer the boat. He heard the sound of distant connecting-rods. And then he called out to his father for the last time. He could see how he finally turned around, steadied himself, bent his knees and clutched the iron lever against the sea.

The wave caught the side of the boat and hurled it like a snooker cue against Cercadas. But the boy, when he remembered, felt no

66

pain. He ran, ran, whirling his arms, down the wing, electrified like the Iron Maiden spectre. He had passed all his opponents, one by one, scored the third goal in extra time, and now he runs in slow motion down the wing, his long hair floating, while the Riazor Blues wave the blue and white flags. He runs down the wing with outstretched arms to embrace the white-haired coach.

HAVANA'S VAST CEMETERY

I also had an uncle in America. And I hope I still do, watering miniature roses in the Galician Pantheon with his zinc bucket.

My uncle's name was Amaro and he had died at least eight times before dying. He was a specialist in dying and he always did so with great dignity. He would come back from death smelling of La Toja soap, his hair combed in the style of the Mallo Orchestra's accordionist, in possession of a new, Prince of Wales check suit and a surprising story. Once he gave a detailed description of the menu at the Heavenly Banquet, where, he said, there was plenty of ham and turnip tops.

"And pig's head as well?" my father asked with irony.

"Absolutely! There was a pig's head on every table, with two sprigs of parsley tucked up its nostrils and a daisy chain."

"What was the weather like?"

"It was cold enough, but sunny. Not like in purgatory. A cruel north-east wind blew in purgatory. It's a moor without trees."

I would put this ability to die without dying completely down to the unusual nature of a cowboy who had blue blood, and Amaro would prove this by breaking his nose on feast days, simply by pinching it with his fingers, like frost. The blue trickles of blood would flow from his nostrils, and he would sip them as a child does mucus.

I think, however, that he had learned to die in Havana's vast cemetery.

"The ocean was still moving under my feet when someone put a broom and a zinc bucket in my hands." This is how he related his first journey, from the village of Mist to the Caribbean. "I was too young to have encountered the cut-throat razor. I followed in the footsteps of Mingos O'Pego, the countryman to whom my parents had entrusted me, and with a broom of palmettos and that gleaming bucket I joined the service corps of Christopher Columbus, the first and foremost cemetery in America. I didn't come out for a month, believe it or not. O'Pego was addicted to rum. He had a whole cellar hidden away in one of the niches of the Galician Pantheon. 'Look at this dead chap,' he said to me, 'hee, hee!' And he gave me a clear warning, 'You'd better not lay a finger on him, eh, lad?' He was due to find me a room in the parish of the living, but meanwhile I worked there all day and slept there, in a small hut in the cemetery, between wreaths of flowers and marble crosses. There I learned to distinguish voices and music that the rest couldn't hear."

I would huddle up in Amaro's lap and my fear seemed to spur him.

"What nights in Havana's cemetery! Indians, Negroes, Galicians! Drums and bagpipes! Everyone dancing in the warm night, while O'Pego snored on a pillow of roses and carnation wreaths! We had a cat which grew and grew in the night to the size of an ocelot or jaguar, and scoffed down huge rats like hares, hee, hee! *La Habana, Habanita mía,* how pretty everything is in Havana! Even being a gravedigger in Havana was pretty!"

My parents ran a bar on Orzán Street in Coruña, which was so close to the sea that the ocean sometimes bubbled up into the toilet. The customers were regulars, so regular that their drinking bowls were numbered. Amaro's was number 36. Unusually, my uncle drank in small sips, delicately, solemnly drawing the white porcelain cup towards him. Then, with misty eyes, he would contemplate the dregs of Ribeiro wine, like someone observing a dramatic piece of embroidery. "The world! If only you knew what a small place the world is, child!"

"Oy, you, fish-face, tell me! Which is older, Hercules Tower or Santiago Cathedral?" asked bowl number 7 at the bar.

"I don't give a daaamn about anything!" bowl 9 proclaimed.

> *All of the clouds, they are weeping*
> *on account of a love that has died.*
> *All of the streets, they are gleaming*
> *from the rain that has fallen tonight.*

A sailor was singing who had no numbered bowl and had arrived trailing a storm that he left on the doorstep, whining like an abandoned dog.

"Quieten down, animal!" said bowl number 3, something of a recluse who had merged with the old pinewood table and had cobwebs dangling from his eyes.

"Was that directed at me?" the sailor asked challengingly, puffing out his chest.

"Excuse me, sir," my Uncle Amaro intervened opportunely, "do you happen to know Havana?"

"Havana? Like the back of my hand!" he shouted from the bar. He then drew near, prompted by curiosity. "Havana, good heavens, the beauty of Havana! My heart misses a beat just saying the word!"

"And mine hurts," sighed Uncle Amaro. "And the Christopher Columbus cemetery? Do you know Havana's vast cemetery?"

"No, I can't say I do. I was set on a different course!"

"Shame. I was the official head gardener there," my uncle explained with a real sense of pride.

"Chrysanthemums are good for the dead," said bowl number 5.

"I prefer dahlias!" proclaimed the next.

"You're drunk!" shouted a recluse who could not stand up, after a long drink.

"Is it long since you left?" enquired the sailor.

71

"It was at the time of the Revolution. I was poor, but I had a gold tooth, and someone arrived shouting that the Revolution would rob me of my gold tooth. I still have it." He opened his mouth to show the false tooth to the sailor, who tilted his head with great interest. "Before I knew it, I'd lost Havana," my uncle said, having polished the tooth with his tongue.

"In these situations," declared the sailor sententiously, "you always end up following the others and sometimes putting your foot in it."

"How much does it cost now to get a gold tooth?" asked bowl number 12.

"The Christmas bonus isn't enough!" said number 7.

"How was Havana when you came away?" my uncle enquired unhappily.

"In need of a lick of paint . . . and pretty."

"Just how I left her." And then he cheered up, "Let's strip the Ribeiro's rose of its petals in her memory!"

My father was not amused by these rounds for which no one paid. Amaro did not have a penny to his name and always died after toasting Havana. This is exactly what happened. Fed up with his comings and goings from one world to the next, this time my parents did not arrange a wake, there was no soap, no combing his hair, no suit.

"Stay there," my father commanded, "and tell us when he comes back."

I fell asleep beside him, but when I woke up he was cold and looked like he would never come back from that journey. He wore a pained smile and, in his half-open mouth, the gold tooth was missing. He has yet to return from that crossing. There's no doubting they put him in a niche in the village of Mist, but I imagine him in Customs somewhere, trying to pay for the ticket with his tooth in the palm of his hand like a precious grain of corn, negotiating a return to Havana's vast cemetery.

THE GIRL WITH THE
PIRATE TROUSERS

One of them had succumbed to the temptation to whistle quietly
for a few seconds and then he himself looked around as if searching for the guilty crevice where the wind had whistled. The other
recognized the melody and followed it through the roof, till the
wings of his eyes beat against the poor, sleepy light.

> Green laurel, out of the way,
> let the light of the moon through,
> I'm sitting up on the hillside
> and can see nothing with you.

But he did not open his mouth. Had he done so, had he hummed
the tune, it would have sounded like an accusation. In the same
way, he said nothing about the unmentionable pain of the water's
needle in his temple, the relentless dripping of the tap in the
derelict basin. Concealing his anguish, he placed a cloth underneath
which muffled the tinkle, but the liquid burst of pellets had already
bored a hole in his head.

The two of them smoked dark tobacco. There was an empty,
crushed cigarette packet which had now the irregular roundness
of a flat, leather ball left in the corner of a damp changing room.

The two of them had been goalkeepers. This was all they had
confided to each other in five, long days, which seemed like years.
Of course, they had not said for which team or which parish. The

coincidence had made them glance at one another, raising their eyebrows with a mixture of surprise and fascination. It would have been rash to carry on with that conversation. To know that they smoked the same tobacco was as far as their intimacy could go. They were comrades and they had a mission to fulfil. This was as much as they needed to know about each other.

A map bound them together. The rest was false. Their names, occupations, origins. Even their fingertips had been treated with acids to erase their identity.

There was the map, on top of the table, next to the zinc pan containing the burnt-out cigarettes like the dross of night. Nothing else should reveal that they had been there. In the last hour, they smoothed out the blankets on the beds, as if dispelling the aura of the bodies that had slept there.

The two of them had, in effect, been goalkeepers. Someone, somewhere, had chosen them and perhaps this had been the deciding factor. Because he, whoever he was, knew everything about them, a hidden camera in their lives. Without a doubt, he imagined them like this, as they were, silent, accustomed to long periods of time on their own and eternally alert, even when the ball was far away, in the other area. Restful and solid, but also feline, on the lookout, muscles at the ready, springs that would uncoil without fail at the critical moment.

They each looked at their watch and nodded, having themselves fallen into line during their lengthy confinement like the internal gears of a time machine and feeling in their bones the mechanical rotation of the teeth of History.

It was time.

They collected all the remains, starting with the map, and burnt them one by one in the minimal fire of retreat.

It was definitely midday.

After the long night of five days, they were blinded by the

sunlight, put on their guard by the metallic singing of the crickets, a deafening, hidden army that seemed to have been waiting for them on the ground. Soon, however, they set out resolutely, reducing the world to the lines of the map printed on their mind. There, to the left, between two laurel hedges, was the short cut, the old track where carts had rolled in previous years, which was now carpeted with bracken and fallen leaves. They advanced like divers on the soft sea bottom, trying to make the flight of the birds as silent as that of fish.

Rather than having anything to do with men, this mission seemed to have been devised by nature's murky imagination. Even the racket of the crickets reminded them now of friendly infantry fire. Everything had been disposed, drawn up, dreamed of, in the past. Labourers with iron arms like ploughshares had dug that deep path many years ago because someone, in a dream steaming with manure, saw that this would be the vegetal tunnel along which the two brave men who were going to kill the Beast would travel.

In this way, protected from the sun and inquisitive eyes, they reached the old, deserted mill fenced off with tall brambles. The coarse vegetation, however, caressed them like velvet. They sensed it was on their side. The map was accurate. The millstones were two circles sketched in stone and, in the wall, the draughtsman had opened up the exact window, with its panes of glass lined with dust and cobwebs. It was the best, the most discreet, viewpoint possible. At a short distance, sharp and splendid, seemingly drawn by the same hand that had designed the map, was the bridge. Even the sentries, standing one at either end, seemed to want to copy the stiffness of the strokes with which they had been marked down on the paper.

Underneath the window, on the ground, concealed by a layer of moss, were the ends of the cables. The Beast and his retinue were due to pass by in half an hour. At that precise moment, all they had to do was complete the electric circuit and the bridge would crumble like a child's Meccano.

With an eye on the time, they took turns to keep watch, while the other remained silent and stonelike, leaning against the wall. There was hardly any traffic across the bridge. Occasionally, a car would slow down, intimidated by the checkpoint, or a tractor towing a stack of grass, with the lazy gait of farm machinery in the heat. Time passed slowly as well, held back by the buzzing of the insects and the explosion of the broom's pods. At five minutes to the hour, according to the routine indicated on the map, the sentries would stop the traffic and order the drivers over, leaving the bridge clear.

That moment had yet to arrive and now it was a girl passing by on her bicycle, followed by three pairs of eyes taken captive as if they wanted to fill the place of the wheels. Her hair was fastened in a long ponytail and she wore a blouse with balloon sleeves and a pair of tight, black, pirate trousers, which reached to her knees. The two sentries and the look-out hidden in the mill watched as the girl turned her head towards the river, stopped pedalling and then put one foot on the ground to come to a halt. She rested the bicycle against the bridge and placed her elbows on top of the parapet.

Since the arrival of the cyclist's slender figure, the look-out in the mill had remained outside reality. This presence did not figure on the map. There was no line to represent the figure of a woman leaning on the parapet, contemplating the flow of the river, nor two circles like wheels to indicate the exact spot, halfway across the bridge, where the main pier was and, stuck to it, the explosive charge. He remained a few seconds longer, enchanted by the young cyclist's graceful beauty, unable to establish a link between the apparition's unreality and the hands of his watch. On the contrary, he was more inclined to marry the image with the beds of clover and wild strawberry that could be glimpsed under the alders, at the bends in the river. But something was not right. He felt an unpleasant cramp in his stomach when he looked down and saw the cables that joined him so closely to her.

He attracted the attention of his colleague, who required more precious seconds to assimilate reality's mistake, that absurd doll on the stage of History.

"What the fuck's she doing?"

"Nothing. Looking at the river."

"Why don't they fucking move her?"

"You're right. They're supposed to. The reports said they never allow anyone on the bridge."

"They're stopping the traffic. For fuck's sake, why don't they say anything to her?"

They had five minutes before ridding themselves of the Beast. For a long time now, for years, the Organization had prepared with maximum secrecy the coup that would send him to hell. Hundreds of eyes had spied the tyrant's movements until they had discovered a weak point, the bridge on a secondary road, in his cobweb without routines. After that, a lot of people had risked their neck without knowing or wanting to know, striking the ball like static players in table football, controlled by an unknown someone, somewhere, surveying the whole at a sufficient height. All that warp, that web of anonymous wills now depended on them.

The man writing was also now looking out of the window, smoking the dark tobacco that they were forbidden at this critical hour in history.

His daughter, a small girl aged eight, opened the door.

"What are you doing?"

"I'm writing a story."

"Is it a children's story?"

"No. It's for adults."

"Oh! You always say you're going to write children's stories and then you never do."

"When I finish this one, I'll write a story for children. I promise."

"That's what you always say."

The man writing looked at his watch and then searched for a bridge over a river, beyond the landscape of roofs with seagulls and terrace roofs with clothes hanging out to dry.

"Listen," he said to the girl. "There's a bad man, a very bad man, who runs a country as if it were a prison and sometimes kills those who protest. He has a lot of power, and a lot of guards who do what he tells them. This man, whom people secretly call the Beast, is about to cross a bridge in a car. Under that bridge is a very large bomb. But then, on the bridge, something happens. A girl appears riding a bicycle, stops pedalling and starts looking at the river . . ."

"And?"

"Well. The men with the bomb don't know what to do."

"That's silly! What they have to do is . . ."

Suddenly, the man writing looked with terror out of the window. The glass rattled and dull thunder exploded inside his head, frightening the seagulls away. He cursed under his breath.

"What's wrong?" the girl asked.

"Nothing. It's late already," he said, looking at his watch. "Time for pretty young girls to be in bed."

CONGA, CONGA

The sunlight hurt his eyes. It came in through the blinds, sharp as a scythe's blade. He looked at the alarm clock with a pained, incredulous expression. The clock's daggers were fighting a duel. Ana had gone without saying goodbye and left a void full of reproach on the bed.

He noticed the oily, sugary sweat of alcohol on his skin. It was so late he felt the ancient sense of shame of an idle farmer. He stepped into the shower and turned the cold water on full. He hoped it would wash away everything, all the slimy, yesteryear music that the night had left him. A party of old friends. Like fools, all of them chewing on the fuchsia leaves of a lost Eden.

Ana had left a note on the kitchen table with the address and precise details. A house in Mera. The boy's name's Óscar. He's nine years old. They're moneyed. Three hours, at 5,000 pesetas/hour: 15,000 pesetas. Plus 2,000 pesetas travel expenses. Total: 17,000 pesetas.

He searched in vain for a mark of affection on the paper. It wasn't even signed. A second reproach.

He grabbed some carrots from the fridge and started nibbling them anxiously. *Create the new rabbit.* Whenever he was hung-over, he took it out on the dumb dreamer he had inside him. The dumb dreamer who, however, always got his own way. It was he who put six rings in his ear and tattoos on the back of his hands. It was he who bought the Yamaha instead of a car, as Ana had wanted. And it was he who kept getting him tangled up like a bramble in every mess that came along.

The dumb dreamer's worst enemy was Ana. She would look him straight in the face and say, "For God's sake! When are you going to grow up?"

He had just enough time. He put on the clown's clothes and rode his motorbike along the coastal road, towards Mera. It was funny. It was always the same. The adults who were driving would look at him severely, as if they felt they were being ridiculed. The others, no. Young and old, sitting in the back of cars or on buses, would wave, laugh, or pretend to shoot with their hands.

At the front door of the house, there was one of those entry-phones with a camera. He pressed the button and stared into the camera's dark eye. They still asked who he was and he responded very seriously.

"It's me. The clown."

He knew what would happen. In a few seconds, the children would be heard screaming. Like baby seagulls. There was Mother Seagull, looking him up and down. One of those blondes with qualities of leadership.

"This is Óscar. Óscar, say hello to the clown! There, run along now and play! And make sure you behave!"

Pico, the clown, broke into a hop.

> Everyone who's at this party,
> go ahead and have some fun.
> If you want to soon be laughing,
> copy everything I've done.

"Jump, everyone!" Pico shouted.

And everyone jumped.

"Fly, everyone!"

Óscar and a friend with curls like a blond angel stood with their arms by their sides, whispered something to each other and gave him a mocking look.

"Óscar, come here please," said Pico.

The boy obeyed him unwillingly, with a look of disgust.

"Here, Óscar, this tooth's really hurting me," said Pico, opening his mouth and pointing. "Will you take it out?"

All the boys and girls approached them and watched expectantly.

"It's a bit bigger than the others. Can you see it?"

"Yes, yes," said the boy a little nervously. "But how do you want me to do it?"

"With this!" said Pico, suddenly producing a pair of pincers which he drew out of the bottom of his pocket.

"With this?"

"That's right. Have no fear!"

The boy hesitated before placing the implement in his mouth.

"Do you want someone else to do it?" Pico asked.

In a fit of temper, the boy gripped the pincers and pulled at the tooth so hard that he fell backwards. It was a fake tooth. Everyone burst out laughing. The clown put his hand to his cheek and made a big pretence.

"That's stupid," said Óscar, standing up.

For the next game, the clown made them form a ring. They had to learn a song and dance.

> Conga, conga,
> who can last longer?
> We want to see Pico
> dancing the conga.
> One hand on his head,
> the other on his waist,
> swinging his hips
> like the lady he is.

He repeated the performance three times. He danced gracefully and the children, especially the girls, clapped their hands.

"Right. Now it's Óscar's turn."

"No, I don't want to," said the birthday boy.

"Óscar, Óscar!" everyone shouted.

"Come on, cheer up!" said the clown, adopting a slightly serious tone. "Why don't you want to?"

"It's a sissies' game!" the blond angel laughed.

"Yeah, it's for sissies!" said Óscar.

The clown turned around and asked who wanted to go first. The kids seemed at a loss. Finally, a girl raised her hand.

"What's your name?"

"Ana."

"Ana, is it? Wonderful! Come on, all together now!"

> *Conga, conga,*
> *who can last longer?*
> *We want to see Ana*
> *dancing the conga . . .*

On hearing the clapping, some of the grown-ups came and danced as well. Pico watched out of the corner of his eye. Óscar and the blond angel were smiling contemptuously and gave the distinct impression that they were up to something.

"Come, Óscar!" he called out in a friendly spirit. "Now we're going to do something you'll like. A sack race!"

"That's dumb!" Óscar exclaimed.

"That clown is just boring!" said the blond angel for his part.

Pico pretended not to hear. Instead, he put his feet in a sack and started bounding with so much suppressed rage that he looked as if he were going to fly straight over the cypress hedge like one of those characters in novels. His fall was greeted with roars of laughter all round. Of course, that was the point, he thought, to carry on falling that the others might feel on the vertical line of happiness.

"Clown!"

It was Óscar calling out to him. He seemed more contented.

"Clown, come this way, please. I want to show you something you'll like."

"Come on, kiddies. Let's follow Óscar!"

"No, no," said the boy. "Just you. It's a surprise. Everyone else can come later."

Pico sensed that something was not right. The little brat was probably playing out one of those stupid films with repugnant children, such as *Home Alone* or something. But there was nothing for it but to keep going and see where the matter ended.

"This way, this way!"

Óscar opened the door of a sort of conservatory, made out of aluminium and glass.

"Listen, Óscar . . ."

The boy suddenly jumped outside and closed the door behind him. Pico struggled, but Óscar, with a sinister smile, slid the bolt across. "Bastard," murmured the clown, "little shit".

"Open up, Óscar! Please!"

But the lad pressed his nose to the glass. Next to him, wearing the same sinister smile, was the blond angel.

The summer-house was full of huge, exotic-looking plants. The warmth was humid, and it was like being inside a vegetal sauna. He had come across worse inventions. He decided to sit down. Let the little brats have a rest. It was then that his sixth sense, what he called his Inner Detector, began to whistle like mad. He looked around without noticing anything special until he became aware that one of the rubber trees was looking at him as well. He muttered an imprecation.

For some time he had been used to the idea that his dress as a self-employed worker was that of a clown. But now he felt as out of place as if he were running naked through the rainforest. Remain calm, Pico, don't shout, he thought. Things can get worse. No, it doesn't look like a crocodile. It must be a cayman.

In spite of their appearance, they're very swift. When they attack, they're as quick as lightning. They sink their teeth in and don't let go. Et cetera.

Very slowly, without looking away, he stood up on the chair. It was then that he shouted.

"Help, help!"

Why was he shouting? He should be keeping quiet.

"Help, help!"

His legs were trembling. He had never felt so afraid. All the children were pressing against the glass. Very funny. A cartoon film. Little shits.

Finally, the blonde with qualities of leadership appeared, took him into the house and offered him something to revive his spirits. Yes, he'd love a scotch.

"You and I need to have a talk," his mother had said to her little Óscar.

Hard as steel. That criminal in the making didn't even seem to hear. He ran off with the blond angel to play at killing people.

"Boys will be boys!" she said. "Still, you'll be used to it."

"Sure. I get it virtually every day. When it's not a cayman, it's a boa constrictor."

She smiled. Clever girl.

She showed him the bathroom so that he could remove his make-up and change his clothes. He thanked her for it. Today, the character really weighed quite heavily on him. He wanted to see that sticky mask wash down the drain.

When he was in the shower, hidden behind the screen, he heard someone opening the door and coming in. So it was them! Óscar and the blond angel had come to do a pee. He leapt out of the shower and hastened to slide the bolt across so that they could not leave.

They looked at him in amazement. Who was this guest and what was he doing there naked, wearing only a sinister smile?

"You're two very, very naughty children," said Pico very slowly, in a sarcastic tone.

They recognized him and laughed nervously. There was something unsettling about the way he spoke. The clown's face was pale, with remnants of white paint under his eyes, and his chest was as hairy as a gorilla's.

"Do you know what happens to naughty, naughty children? Don't you?"

Pico now stopped imitating Jack Nicholson as the Joker in *Batman*. He adopted the solemn voice of God on the Day of Judgement.

"Well, naughty, naughty children are sent to hell!"

Óscar and the blond angel tittered in horror. They tittered the way naughty, naughty children titter shortly before falling through the trapdoor of hell.

THE OBJECTS

"He wasn't a very expressive member of the audience, that much is true," said the Television. "He would sit there, on the couch, with a glass of whisky, and watch coldly, as if it were only the ice cubes that had gone to his head. That night was different. That night, he moved his lips in time to the character on the screen. It was as if he were at a dubbing session. And I don't think he liked what he said. Or what he saw. He made gestures, like someone looking at themselves misshapen in a fairground mirror who wants to accentuate their ugliness."

Contrary to custom, the Television thought for a few seconds.

"OK, I accept that this last remark of mine is conditioned by what has happened."

"He didn't read much," said the Hamlet lying on the sitting-room table. "At least, not in the latter years. But that night, that night he came towards the shelf and all the books, we started nudging each other. He touched various spines, but in the end he picked me. He read as far as act three scene two at a stretch, and left a mark here, on the page where it says that bit about *Let me be cruel, not unnatural.*"

"Clear as daylight," said the Glass in a hoarse voice.

"Why?" the Lamp asked.

"What do you mean, why? That's the explanation you're looking for."

"Don't be dumb," the Lamp retorted, projecting shadows like

black swans. "*Let me be cruel, not unnatural!* When it comes to it, that could be read in a variety of ways. Besides, with all due respect for our friend Hamlet here, it is not something that a detective can present these days as proof before a judge. A verse only implicates its author, and not even that. All he left written in his own handwriting was a note for the cleaning lady, 'Please give the window in the sitting-room a go.' Not exactly what I would call a dramatic farewell."

"But one of the policemen, the fattest one, made a note," said Hamlet shyly. "He opened at the mark and wrote in his notebook."

"I could read what he wrote," said the Lamp ironically. "*My tongue and soul in this be hypocrites.* That's what he noted down. Your problem, my friend, is that everyone sees what they want to see."

"The girl was very clever," said the Ashtray with the pride of someone who knows too much. "She removed all trace. She even put the butt with the lipstick in her handbag."

"She didn't do it!" shouted the Television in a state of agitation.

"How can you be so sure?" the Wall Clock asked. "No one had ever looked at me like that. Wearing the expression of a bad epitaph, as Hamlet would say."

"She was furious, that's all," said the Television. And then added in a low voice, "I know her very well. She'd never do it. She'd never actually do it . . ."

The Clock laughed like someone with experience of the world.

"We saw her shoot inside you once. Why wouldn't she do so outside? She was as fond of films in real life as on the screen. Do you remember the love scenes there, on the couch? Break me, eat me, kill me!"

"You're dumb," the Television interrupted. "You don't understand a thing."

"I'm realistic," the Clock carried on unperturbed. "We all know what happened. It's people who don't. People will swallow whatever

88

you tell them. But there's no changing what happened. She was jealous. And she was right to be. She discovered that the other woman had been here. The other woman was in the air. They went to the bedroom. They argued. And there was a weapon. She knew that there was a weapon on the bedside table. She shot and killed him. As in the film. Why deceive ourselves? We all heard what the Pistol was saying."

"You're quite right," the Lamp agreed.

"We didn't see anything," said the Television. "We didn't actually see anything."

"We heard and that's enough!" shouted the Clock.

"Stop bullying!" replied the Television angrily.

It was raining outside with the sad percussion of film noir. Neon tears slid down the window. The Clock, domineering, measured the suspense. Then spoke calmly.

"We all heard what the Pistol said, 'It was her! It was her!'"

But then, with a voice from the beyond, out of the bedroom, the Darkness shouted,

"The Pistol is a cynic!"

All the objects waited expectantly, with the Clock's pulse drumming in the temples of the house.

"When the girl ran towards him to embrace him," the Darkness recounted, "I heard the Pistol murmur, 'Were it not for me, you'd never ditch this bum!'"

They waited for Hamlet to have the last word. But he was looking out over the harbour. The siren of a boat from Sole greeted the god of day, like a sea cock.

CARTOONS

To the Ninja turtles, who taught my children how to say,
"Cowabunga!"

"Come, Mary, this is our sponsor," said Thanks Danke, smiling from ear to ear. "Mr Miles Townsend."

The smile was about as genuine as a flight attendant's. The only natural thing was the chimpanzee white of the palm of his hands.

"Hello, darling. Charming, Danke, just as I imagined her."

I'd been through a terrible morning. I'd burnt the toast and had a fight with Han Cock. I'd left him for good. All I'd taken were the car keys.

"Danke tells me you're willing to finance a series."

"That's right, darling."

"Do you enjoy cartoons, Mr Townsend?" I asked for the sake of asking.

"They're my passion, darling," he said sarcastically.

"If I'm not mistaken, the main character will have to spend the day eating sausages."

"Something like that. Isn't it a super idea?"

"Pork sausages."

"All the sausages in the world, darling, so long as they're pork. As for the rest," he said, sticking his thumbs up, "absolute freedom!"

"The pay's very good, Mary," Thanks intervened.

"I'm sure it is."

And so Fat Fatty was born, the most repulsive character I could come up with. Miles Townsend's interest in cartoons was not an accident. The new vegetarian sausage had appeared on the market to widespread approval. The impact of this product was not unconnected with the previous launch of a children's series starring Green Grun, who had become a real hero in a couple of weeks. Green Grun posters, stickers, badges, toys, video games and, of course, Green Grun sausages could be seen everywhere. The sponsor of the series was Denaro Money, Miles Townsend's long-standing rival. Although the television companies kept this detail a secret. I know because the scriptwriter was Han Cock, my ex-lover. Townsend and Money competed in everything, but especially in sausages, paintings and women, in that order. One day, they insulted each other at an art auction in Sotheby's and had to be pulled apart by their respective bullies. Townsend was accompanied by Money's ex-wife, an Indonesian ex-model, and Money had Townsend's ex-wife on his arm, a Jamaican ex-model.

Thanks to Fat Fatty, a murderous and unscrupulous hero who fascinated children and ate dozens of sausages after peeing on the corpses and writing "Death to greens" on the walls, I was able finally to buy an attic with a glass roof in an intelligent building located in the Big Apple.

One night, while I was playing chess with my computer, a terrible storm broke out. I had never felt what panic was until then. I went out into the corridor and when I pressed the lift button, I heard an impersonal voice, like that of a stewardess at an airport.

"I'm very sorry, madam, but I can't seem to work."

It was also an intelligent lift. The emergency staircase, for its part, recommended me not to use it. The voice was hoarser than the lift's.

"Dear residents, in the event of an electrical storm, please do not leave your homes," said another voice, in the unmistakable clinical tone of those that terrorize when they're trying to sound reassuring.

Back in the attic, I discovered that someone, at last, had taken an intelligent decision. The vast vault of the roof had been closed, freeing me from the warlike clamour of the heavens. But now, against the metal cover, the hail rang out with a machine gun's ire. This was more than I could take. There I was, defenceless before the inclement attack of the international terrorist par excellence, the one they call Gaia, perfidious Nature, cursed Mother Earth, and right in the heart of the most metropolitan metropolis in the civilized world. With a mixture of resentment and longing, I remembered Han Cock. He'd been around. He'd even appeared in a cigarette ad and written a *Patriotic Guide* to childhood before turning himself over to cartoons. I called him, naturally.

"Rest assured, darling. I'll be there in ten minutes."

"The building's intelligent. It might not let you in."

"Don't worry. I've dealt with these pups before."

For a moment, I imagined that Han would come riding on the back of a bolt of lightning and fall down in front of me, with a stainless steel smile. I was dead pleased when I heard the doorbell very soon afterwards. It was Han, my own Han Cock. I couldn't avoid throwing myself into his arms. But, once he'd groped around and given me an animalistic kiss, he flung me violently on to the sofa.

"Bitch. You'd like to finish me off."

"But, what are you saying, Han?"

"You know what I mean."

I'd never seen him like this. His eyes were full of hatred. My instinct told me he was not joking. He seemed to have lost all control.

"I'll kill you, Mary."

"Cock, darling. You're my only true love."

"It's not about that, you sexy rodent."

It struck me as an amusing compliment, but now was not exactly the time to be laughing.

"You know what I mean," he repeated. "You're going to eat all of these on your own. One by one."

Heavens above! It was a super-family pack of Fat Fatty sausages.

"You know? They're calling me a failure and they're going to cancel the Green Grun series on account of your greasy, disgusting, pissing, green-killing murderer!"

"Listen, Cock . . ."

"I never thought you'd get back at me in this way, you perverse whore."

"Listen, Cock. I hate Fat Fatty!"

"Eh?"

"That's right. I hate that slimy pig and I'll kill him if you ask me to. There'll be no more Fat Fatty stories."

"Are you sure about that?"

"I swear, Cock."

Gradually, he calmed down. Then we kissed on the sofa and ended up rolling about the floor. At the end of the combat, we sat down, feeling relaxed. I realized that the bullets had stopped falling on the roof and drew back the vault.

"Ah, Mary, ain't that just beautiful?" he exclaimed with the voice of John Wayne on the prairie, on a starry night.

"Thanks to Fat," I said in a way that he wouldn't find irritating.

He laughed.

"You're a great scriptwriter, Mary. If I let you, you'd finish me off."

I told him I was going to make some dinner for my love. I entered the kitchen and went straight to the fridge. I had a good supply of Green Grun sausages. And, in the pantry, some devastatingly fast poison pills.

A WHITE FLOWER FOR BATS

To Camilo Nogueira

The old man fondled the boy roughly, pinching him like a hunting dog on the back of the neck. Then he lifted him up by the shoulders and dropped him into the dark, foul-smelling crypt of the cask.

"Go for it, Dani. Get rid of that filth!"

The small boy was holding a bucket of water and a broom. He scrubbed the smooth surfaces and then, conscientiously, at the old man's insistence, the joins of the oak staves and the furthest corners, there where the lees settle, the remains of the last fermentation, like a foul, putrid lichen. When the old man, at a prearranged signal, moved the cask, the boy felt as if he were rolling inside the bowels of a giant, ancient animal, such as dozes in the imagination of humid, leafy woods and, when it has its belly tickled, slowly turns over.

"Go for it, Dani, till there's nothing left!"

The brush scraped off the crust of dirt and the water unearthed the memory of the wood's aroma. In the beginning, he had felt a sharp twinge in his nose. As evening closed in, he sniffed at the cracks and crevices, in search of the last sediment. He heard the old man's murmur like a litany handed down from his forebears: a speck of dirt can spoil the finest vintage. His grandfather's was a small vineyard, Corpo Santo, no more than one hundred vines, but it was one of the jewels of the Ribeiro region, a blessed plot of land that brought pride to their lineage. It produced an enviable wine, the best friend you can find.

"That's the boy, Dani! Polish it up like an angel's bottom!"

A man's homeland is his childhood. The Lord gives us all different qualities. Some develop them and others allow them to go to waste. The Lord gave me a broom and an innate ability to detect filth. I can smell it a mile away and God well knows that, insofar as I am able, I'll give it a good clean wherever I find it.

Here's the story of how my nose works. The guard-boat zig-zagged in between the mussel-beds in the Arousa estuary. Suddenly, I notice the characteristic itch, my nose moves like a compass. I signal to the pilot, who slows the boat down. The sea is calm and rumbles in time to the engine. The whole shore is a string of fairy lights. Atlantis. But the crew scan the nearest mussel-bed, as if we had arrived at a phantasmagorical palafitte or prehistoric settlement.

"Now!"

The boat's powerful searchlight cuts the night in two. A flock of seagulls, indignant at being woken up, assails us with insults. On the large raft, piles of seaweed take shape sluggishly, thick ropes returned by the sea with clusters of shells. More than masts, the logs tautening the cables look like survivors of a primitive power line. The eyes follow the searchlight. There is a wooden cabin with a thatched roof. A wetsuit hangs like a skin of plastic. My nostrils distend as the searchlight pans to the end of the platform.

"There, point it there, Fandiño!"

I jump out of the boat and skip across the rafters. The hatch is too big for a floating tank, as if it were a submarine or something. I wrestle with my hands, trying to open it, but my nose puts me on my guard. I shout to the men to hurry up with the torch and a crowbar. With one push on the crowbar, I lever up the lid. Shit! The dark hole starts spitting out shots compulsively and we hurl ourselves on to the rafters. Inches from my face, the sea splashes about like a happy idiot.

"Over to you, Fandiño."

Fandiño's voice booms out like that of a heartless janitor at the Last Judgement.

"Listen up, shitheads! There are thousands of hungry flatfish down there just waiting to tuck into the pricks of some fresh corpses! Prick-eating flatfish! Eye-popping crabs! Ball-sucking octopuses! So why don't you come on up with sparks flying out of your arses and your balls in the air? Do you hear, bastards? We're going to put the whole artillery down that hole. Do you understand? You won't even get a write-up in the newspapers! Your families will remember you every time they open a tin of food!"

"That's enough, fat boy," I say to Fandiño. "Police! One minute!"

There is no need to wait.

"What is that?"

An incredibly small figure appears in the hatchway. As small as a child.

"For Christ's sake!" exclaims Fandiño, removing his finger from the trigger. "If it's not a child!"

The figure sways as it tries to stand up on the logs, as if the strength of the searchlight had splintered its bamboo legs. It is thin as a slice of cod.

"Was it you shooting?"

"I was frightened. Very frightened, si . . . sir," it says with a stutter.

Fandiño goes down the hole and comes back out again very quickly.

"There's enough white stuff here to feed a million noses!"

"What's your name?" I ask the boy.

"Sebastião."

Sometimes they do this. While they're waiting to pick up the merchandise, they leave a guard on the platforms. There are robberies between them. This job goes to the poor sod at the back. Stuck in there for days on end, enough to drive him crazy. But, Jesus! I don't remember anything like this before. He's only a child!

"Right, Sebastião, do you know something? I'm going to do your job."

So off goes the boat and I stay behind, stuck in the tank. I am very patient. I watch myself growing a beard. Until I hear the rumble of an engine. I prepare the gun. But, suddenly, my nose tells me to get the hell out of there. When I finally manage to open the hatch, I can hardly see for the smoke. Doused in fuel, the mussel-bed is burning like a sacrifice in the middle of the estuary.

That was the first time I heard Don's hearty laugh. I'm sure he wasn't there, but I heard him roaring with laughter. He laughed at me often and sometimes to my face. The last time, I remember it very well, it was at the White Elephant in Lisbon. I had grown another beard while waiting for him. I was sure that on this occasion I was at last going to photograph him with the other Don, all the way from America. I had worked for weeks deciphering codes, interpreting telephone messages, searching for the meaning of absurd conversations. It was a small thing – "The white elephant sends his regards to St Anthony" – that gave me the clue. Suddenly, I was asking, "When the hell is St Anthony's day?" But something, someone, caused him to change plans. Don left the White Elephant with a shapely mulatto girl. They passed by my table, his fingers tapping out the music on those sovereign buttocks, right in front of my nose. Shortly afterwards, my car came off the motorway to Oporto. The brakes did not work. A DIY job.

My ambition has always been, with my broom, to reach the filth at the top. It's not an easy task and it's pretty thankless. You'll often find it where you least expect. In the offices with the spotless carpet. Even in the odd superior's. The stink comes out from under

the door, spreads along the corridors and seeps down the telephone lines. You cope until the stench becomes unbearable. Like
the sewage in a septic tank.

"I'm being sold, boss. There's something here that smells bad,
very bad."

"What are you insinuating?"

"Well, it's not exactly my socks."

"This time, I didn't hear you. You're getting a transfer. And, do
you want some advice? Relax a bit."

You win some, you lose some. You just have to accept. I got put
behind a desk, in front of a typewriter. It was like joining the Red
Cross. From the first moment, and as far as I was concerned, people
were always clear that they had a servant of the public before
them and not a lazy civil-service employee. Good people came into
the world to be screwed around, bad people are out there having
it good. Maybe the Lord wanted it like that to put us to the test,
but, for my part, wherever I might be, I do my best to restore the
balance a little. There are cases of doubt, but my nose, in the end,
never fails me.

Unhappy childhood. Parental lack of understanding. Bad com-
pany. Society, et cetera.

OK, I tell him, you could have started going to Mass, right?
Instead of screwing people. I know a lad who's a bell-ringer. His
father, a drunk. His mother, no one knows. He gets up early every
Sunday and goes and rings the bells. Why don't you ring bells?
I know another who's cross-eyed and specializes in stopping
penalties. Why don't you stop penalties? And there are lots of
other lads who love nature and go hill-walking to observe the
wonders of life, robins and things like that. Did you know there are
white flowers that open up in the night for bats?

On the other hand, a small evil can cause serious damage. So,
the first rule is: never underestimate a case. I've always tried to act

according to this principle and have carved out a certain name for myself with the silent majority.

For example.

An old woman comes into the police station at four o'clock in the morning. A taxi brought her to the door. She must have been a pretty lady. She wears an overcoat that no doubt was elegant 40 years ago, leans on a stick and, even so, as she walks drags her feet as if the ground were covered in snow. She's obviously well known on the night watch. Fandiño, who's sharing the same shift, makes the typical gesture to me of a screw to his temple. He proceeds to hide behind the trench of unsolved cases. Fandiño's a good guy, but he's a lot more sceptical than I am about the possibilities of virtue in the realm of evil. Especially since he got married and had to support a family. I look back with nostalgia now on our times of action in the estuary, when his powerful voice proved more useful than a smoking cannon. Stuck in the office, he was no more than a dozy fat boy. Without so much as a word, the old woman knocks with her stick on the counter. I'd have said she had beautiful, blue eyes were they not bulging, the enamel cracked, and set deep in two dark wells.

"How may I help you, madam?" I say to her with my best smile.

She left the stick with its handle in the shape of a horse on the counter and searched for a handkerchief in her handbag. She was crying now. Her eyes recovered the lustre they had lost. Tears are the best eye-drops in the world. Her elongated hands trembled like the skeletons of herons in the rain.

Well, I'm not the kind of person who says, "Calm yourself, madam". If someone needs to get upset, what better place than a police station? A good cry gives a certain order to the universe, on the threshold of good sense.

"He's going to drive me crazy, he'll finish me off," she said after drying her tears and combing her fingers through her hair.

"What's this about, madam?"

"You appear to be a good person, inspector."

"I am, madam."

"You see? I understand youth."

"Quite."

"I was carefree once myself, you know?" she said with a melancholy smile.

"I'm sure of that, madam."

"You see? I can't sleep. I take pills. Valium, Tranxilium . . . All that. But, oh, God! I have the sensation he's going to come, force the door without my realizing, and enter the bedroom, and then with that horrible knife for killing pigs . . ."

"Come, madam, it's all right!"

"You don't know how terrible he is. How utterly evil he is. He's, he's . . ."

"Who is, madam?" I ask with real interest.

Her look had cracked again, like a pane of glass that's been hit by a stone. She gestured to me to come closer and whispered in my ear,

"Tony. Tony Grief. He wants to kill me, sir!"

I looked around for Fandiño, but he had become absorbed in a crossword.

"So someone wants to murder you and you know who it is."

"Haven't you heard of Tony Grief? Don't tell me you haven't heard of Tony Grief. Of course, that's how the police work!"

The old woman's voice was getting louder. She was cross. She picked up the stick again and it might be said she brandished it in a threatening fashion. I looked back over at Fandiño. He winked at me from behind the trench. By this time, the old lady's stick was rat-tatting on the counter.

"Don't you watch the television? How do you expect to catch any criminals if you don't? Why don't you have a television set here?

What's the use of so many pieces of paper? Is that what we pay our taxes for?"

"Tony Grief," said Fandiño, finally bothering to lend a hand, "is in *Time of Chrysanthemums*. A pretty fruity series."

"Do you know something, madam? If there's one kind of outlaw I hate," I said vehemently, "it's the kind that doesn't let lonely old ladies get some sleep."

My interest threw her. Judging by Fandiño's reaction, it can't have been the first time she had come to the police station to lodge a complaint. Most probably, on previous occasions, they'd recommended she change her television set.

"Don't you have anyone who can help you? Don't you have any children?"

"I have a son. But, you know, he's always very busy."

"I'll tell you what we're going to do. First of all, we'll lodge a formal complaint against this individual, Tony Grief, for which you'll need to fill out this form. With good reason, you'll say what the hell use is a piece of paper when there's a life at stake, but, as I'm sure you know, there's a heap of parasites for whom forms are a raison d'être. Once we've gone through the procedure, which will justify my leaving this hole, we'll head straight to your home and have it out with that shit-head. Tell me, what makes you think that your life is in danger?"

For a moment, I thought that the old woman was going to come to her senses. It tends to happen with people who lose their mind. When you go mad with them, instinct makes them recover their usual health. It's a law of physics, as with communicating vessels. But, to my amazement, I soon learned that it wouldn't work this time. The old woman looked at me in raptures. At last, she had found a partner who could rise to the occasion.

"Listen here, I had that Tony Grief under control. I'm not crazy. Everything was fine while he stayed on the screen. I hated him because he's a really obnoxious fellow, but the way you hate the baddy in films. Sure, I used to insult him and threaten him with my stick. But, well, there aren't many people to talk to, you know? And I was always a great talker. I tell the politicians off as well, in the news. I call them fibbers, spongers and things like that. Other characters I take a shine to and blow them kisses from the palm of my hand. But that Grief! I think I overdid it with the insults because, during the final episodes, he would look at me. He'd be pacing down those sinister streets, with the wind whistling like a deranged horse and, suddenly, he stopped, his face partially lit by a streetlamp, and stared at me with his bloodshot eyes."

"Let us suppose that he did, indeed, look at you. But that Tony Grief continued on his way, or didn't he?"

"You believe I'm mad. Do you think I can't tell sarcasm when I hear it?"

Well. She was right to believe I thought she was mad. But it wasn't my intention to make fun of her. The thing is, I was beginning to get a little fed up of this scumbag called Tony Grief.

"Madam, rest assured that I am prepared to get to the bottom of this," I said with all the seriousness in the world.

"The television set broke down."

"What?"

"That's right. Shortly after Tony Grief fixed his repulsive gaze on me, lines appeared all over the screen. I changed channel, but that did nothing. There was no one to spend the night with."

"Well, that is a coincidence."

"Not a coincidence."

"And when was that, madam?"

"A week ago. But, you see? Let me tell you what happened. I didn't sleep that night. I secured all the bolts. There was a shadow roaming the streets. I live on the third floor and I saw it with my own eyes . . . I heard its footsteps with my own ears. The following day, the television set was still broken. I can't start lugging a television set around. So I looked up a repair shop in the phone book and gave them a call so that they would come and fix it."

"What about your son? Why didn't you call your son, madam? That's what sons are for, when you're in a spot of difficulty."

"I did," she said in a sad tone, lowering her eyes. "But my son is very busy. He doesn't even come to the phone."

"And did they fix the television?"

I could see a video-clip of horror in the old woman's eyes. She'd got caught up in this damn mess. As my grandmother, God rest her soul, used to say, her nervous system had gone to her head.

"Well, you see? As I said, I gave the repair shop a call. Not long afterwards, the doorbell rang. I hastened to open. But I was just about to withdraw the bolt when something stopped me. And I asked. I asked who it was."

She fell silent, looking at me. She sought my protection. She was pleading with me to follow her.

"It was Tony Grief," I said in a grave voice.

"Yes," she said. "He replied that he'd come from the repair shop. 'Did you not call for someone to fix a television?' It was his voice. That cynical, cocksure voice. There was no doubt. When he discovered that I wasn't going to open, he became furious. He banged on the door and shouted, 'You doddery old fool, I hope you die!' It was Tony Grief all right."

I think even Fandiño was impressed.

"He'll be back. I am sure he'll be back. And this time he'll smash the door down."

"Right, madam. Here's what we're going to do. I'm going to collect my coat and escort you home. We'll have a look around. How does that seem to you?"

"You're a good man. I realized from the first moment. I said to myself, 'Here's a good man.'"

"Yes, I am a good person," I murmured as I put on my coat.

The lady's flat was in the old part of the city, overlooking the old harbour, O Berbés. The stairs creaked, but it was worth taking the trouble to get there. The view from the window of the estuary of Vigo at night, the cinemascope of the moon above the Cíes Islands, would have awoken the poetic feeling in an arms dealer. It was the ideal place for two lovers to gallop by the sea till dawn.

"It's a lovely place to be happy, madam," I said to her, searching for a light switch inside her head.

"Here, look," she answered, ignoring my comment and pointing me to the living-room.

There was the blessed TV, as on an altar, surrounded by pieces in a domestic museum. On top of lace cloths from Camariñas, framed photographs, candelabra, a clock mounted in a quartz stone, a Barcelos cockerel, a nickel silver granary, an artistic wine-jar from Buño, a silver censer, a Christ of Victory, pilgrims' scallop shells. On the screen, lines, continual interference.

"Do you see? It's been like this for a week."

"Right, madam, I want you to go and rest now. Have a peaceful sleep. I'll keep an eye out in here."

She didn't seem convinced. No doubt she thought I'd be off as soon as she'd gone to bed. So I decided to give a sign.

"Should Tony Grief turn up, he's in for a nasty surprise."

I opened the window, drew out my pistol and shot at the Cíes moon to see if it bled.

"That's what will happen to Tony Grief."

This seemed to persuade her and I think she was already asleep by the time she reached the end of the corridor. I, on the other hand, for some reason, now felt restless. Having smoked a cigarette to the health of the estuary, I sat down on the sofa, opposite the television set, and waited for it to act like a sleeping pill. I think I was already falling when my nose began to itch. It was a low intensity smell, but unsettling. The light from the screen was like the light used for a post-mortem and filled the whole room. For the first time, I noticed the photographs. I leapt up and looked at them closely, one by one. Don with his mother. Don in a soldier's uniform. Don, smiling, with authorities. Don, smiling even more, at the helm of his yacht. Don holding a trophy, in a tie, at the centre of a football team. Don as a child, dressed for his first Holy Communion.

The sleep had done the old lady the world of good. At the breakfast table, she looked at me sheepishly.

"You must forgive me. When night falls, I lose my head."

"Don't worry. I do know what loneliness is like."

I was going to ask her a favour and I knew she couldn't refuse. I wanted her to accompany me somewhere. We got in the car and followed the coastline as far as Arousa. She realized where we were heading, but remained silent. Nor did she say anything when Don was before us, on the porch of his country house in Olinda.

"Look after your mother. She needs you."

I know I'll never stick him in jail. But I felt as good as if I had scrubbed his insides with a broom.

YOKO'S LIGHT

The father had lost his job. They were moving to another city. The last time the father had given up smoking was on Wednesday. He had picked up the packet of Lucky Strike and thrown it into the rubbish bin. Then he had spat on it. Now it was Sunday and, while he held the steering wheel in one hand, the cigarette trembling in his mouth searched anxiously for the electric coals of the car's lighter.

They were listening to the sports commentary on the radio. The father was concerned about the fate of a particular team and began to move the dial about apprehensively. The mother was worried by a sense of foreboding: all the other cars coming in the opposite direction, were flashing their lights in warning along the grey ash of the road. In front of her, secured with her feet, she held a flowerpot containing an azalea. In the back seat, clutching Yoko, the child nervously watched the flight of day on the car's screen, the sun's embers on the horizon's indolent video. He also had a problem. If they did not hurry up, if that cursed city did not appear soon, he would miss the episode of Hell's Kingdom.

The child adored Baby Devil, the little Satan who was the main character of the series. He could draw him just as he was from memory, with very rapid strokes. He would do so on any paper he had to hand, with chalk on the pavement or with a stick on the sand of the beach. At the school that he was now leaving behind, they had organized a Christmas card competition for the children and he had depicted Baby Devil over the Nativity scene, with a star on his trident. He had not been awarded the prize but he now knew how to differentiate between what success was and what it wasn't. Everyone had talked about his card.

"Do you think you could draw something that wasn't Baby Devil?" the teacher had asked.

Thanks to Baby Devil, the child had managed to shake off the nickname of "Grease-ball". He drew a baby dinosaur with round, tender eyes.

"I like it. It's pretty," the teacher said. "May I keep it?"

She never found this out but that small creature smiling in between gigantic flowers was Baby Devil as well, because quite clearly one of the hero's powers was to make himself invisible or transform into any other being. To be exact, Baby Devil ate souls the way someone licks a Camy ice cream or wolfs down a KitKat or bolts a bag of popcorn. He did not have too much trouble in getting rid of his enemies. The worst moment would come when he was about to be strangled with the Ice Princess's mortal plait or pulverized with the Empty Knight's zero ray gun, and then the little Satan would fire missiles from his eyes, tears the size of the bullets in the old Browning .22 which his father carried under his armpit, neutralize the assailant's sentimental controls, introduce a depression in their software and finally eat their soul. This was a particularly exciting part of the programme, since each soul had a surprising form and an exquisite taste, however perverse and disgusting their previous owners had been. For example, the Ice Princess's was an almond fish and the Empty Knight's was the leaf of a lemon tree fried in swan fat. Like all heroes, Baby Devil wanted to get somewhere and for him this mysterious kingdom was the sweetshop where souls were made, but after each adventure, his desire multiplied by the ephemeral delight, he was forced to revisit his aged father, that baker whose feet were never warm and who harboured a terrible secret. He knew where the Royal Supplier of Souls was to be found, but did not wish to disclose its location to his son for fear of losing him for ever.

"They won," said the father cheerily, banging the steering wheel with the palm of his hand. "Tirnanorg won. That's where we're heading."

"Why did we have to be so late leaving?" said the mother. "We're always late leaving."

"Will we definitely be able to see all the channels?" asked the child quietly. He had already been told many times that they would.

"Tomorrow we'll have to find you a school," replied the mother with a sigh.

The night waited in ambush for them to go past the petrol station. Later it was spotted by the child, its face masked with a red cloth, its legs hanging off the trailer of a tractor. The night rhythmically swayed its feet like the pendulum of a handcrafted clock and sent the boy to sleep, huddled up on the back seat, holding Yoko captive in his lap.

The silence woke him with a gust of fresh air, coldly caressing his podgy hands. All the rest of his body was sweating, since he was lying on the bed in his clothes, covered by a blanket, with his father's jacket at his feet. In the sky of the strange bedroom was a staircase of light which came from the half-open blind. He followed the steps with his eyes until he decided to get up and go towards the window. He recognized the family car beside the lamppost, with that scar on its bonnet. On a hoarding nearby was a big advertisement with a man in a miner's helmet, his face smudged, and large letters that said, "What wouldn't I give now for a Paddy?" That was the beer that his father liked. He opened the door and felt his way along the corridor until he had accustomed his eyes. He switched on the light and saw that he was in the kitchen, bare of things and cold, as if the spirit of the fridge, which was open and empty, were wandering about the house, laying its breath on the pale lustre of the tiles and of the aluminium. The only thing alive, with a life as radiant as it was bewildered, was the azalea standing on the table.

Another door that opened gave into the bathroom, where there was nothing that had not already been seen, the nocturnal desolation of a human laboratory abandoned to the muffled sound of the cistern, a murmur, an old song that connected all the flats, all the cities, that the child had ever known, as if there were an endless, underground pipe in the night transmitting that hoarse gurgling from suburb to suburb, to wherever they happened to be. That blind source made him need a pee and, on lifting the toilet cover, the child discovered, floating in the water like an old sin, like a useless concealment that the drain always returns, the father's cigarette butt and the loose threads of tobacco.

Next he came across their bedroom. He stood in the doorway, without turning on the light, watching only the shape of his parents in the bed, listening to them breathing in time, with increasing intensity. He noticed the cold in his feet from the tiled floor, and had the impression that the ghost of the fridge was coming along the corridor, in the form of a violet current with dirty, yellow teeth. He was on the point of running towards that bed. Whenever he saw them like this, embracing, he felt the desire to slip in between them. But he slowly pulled the door to and headed for the last remaining place.

The child ran his eyes over the familiar pieces of luggage, which were strewn on the living-room floor like heavy, sleepy animals that have grown old together during different moves. There, beside them, protected like a puppy, was Yoko, with its smooth, metallic grey back. He searched for a plug and used the remote to tune in to the various channels. What time was it? On the small screen of the portable television, he saw a car chase, a coral reef full of brightly coloured fish, a black and white film in which one man threatened another, "Get her out of here if you don't want me to take her," and a test card with bagpipe music. Baby Devil, the child thought, will be with his father, asleep in his lap, while he tries in vain to keep his feet warm and cures his nostalgia, like the moth, staring into the heart of the flames.

They were face to face. Little Yoko licked the child's cheeks with light, put sparks in his eyes, but he could feel the cold breath of the spirit of the fridge on the nape of his neck. He heard footsteps. Framed in the doorway, the figure of his father appeared, enormous this time, bigger than he had ever seen it.

"Do you know what time it is?" he shouted angrily.

"I can't sleep," the child was slow to respond.

The father came up slowly and finally bent down beside him. The boy had his eyes glued to Yoko.

"You can't sleep?"

"No. I woke up and I can't sleep."

The father placed his hand on the child's head and Yoko's flames flickered on the skin.

"Do you want to come into our bed?" he asked in a low voice.

"Yes," said the child.

"Do you know how old you are?" said the father now, defensively.

The child did not reply. He seemed captivated by something that was happening on the screen. The grey-haired devil looking gaunt and unshaven caressed Baby Devil with his bony, nicotine-stained fingers. Then he turned Yoko off, picked the child up in his arms and gave him a kiss with his bristly muzzle.

THE COMING OF WISDOM
WITH TIME

To Luisón Pereiro

Though leaves are many, the root is one;
Through all the lying days of my youth
I swayed my leaves and flowers in the sun;
Now I may wither into the truth.

W. B. YEATS

Autumn's broom swept Temple Villas furiously. Old M. closed the gate on his garden of nettles, that sombre green that irritated him like a sin because it made him say, "All right, Pa. I'll pull out the weeds tomorrow so that your sempervivums can grow. And yes, I have seen how lovely Mrs O'Leary's blasted rosebushes are looking." So he slid the bolt across like someone setting loose the clapper of a bell and turned uphill, out of breath, untangling his feet from the crumpled lint of the wind.

There was a change of shift at Arbour Hill Prison. Old M. greeted the guard Mr Eyre, a distant relation, it seemed, on the side of those in Galway, who had a brother who was a priest and another – one Bill – who was a troublemaker and was staying right there, so he'd heard, that was the way of things, one on the inside and one on the out. The point was to keep everyone busy.

He expected an evasive grunt in response, but the guard Mr Eyre looked at him attentively and then said in the solemn tone of someone reciting an old psalm,

"Though leaves are many, the root is one."

He also noticed the whirl of dry leaves, the crazed dance of the unsettled scarecrow who spies winter. It twisted and turned across the meadows, in front of the church adjoining the prison, and then made off, in long, sweeping strides, through the middle of the patriots' graves, the tombs in memory of the dead of 1916. Some of the leaves got lost along the way and flew away like startled sparrows.

"Yes, indeed. The root is one," Old M. repeated, very pleased that Mr Eyre should share a remark of this calibre with him.

Mr Eyre now looked even taller and declared with emphasis in his voice, "And night is about to fall."

"Yes, night is about to fall," Old M. agreed, as if he could already feel the cat's claws in his shoulders.

Without further ado, Mr Eyre got in his car and drove off quickly. And night in its entirety, just as he feared, fell on Old M.

He hastened towards Manor Street, seeking refuge in the hustle and bustle, but there on the corner was Options, the hairdresser's, yes indeed, with that blonde girl who cuts hair, enough to make you lose your head, he wouldn't have minded going in, but the barber Mullen, that razor-sharp tongue, gave him the jitters. He could hear him now, "Did you know? Old Big Ears went over to the other side, hee, hee." He'd done that to Tom O'Grady, and he drove lorries, and he, Old M., laughing at the joke just in case he thought . . . And the thing is when he referred to the hairdressers, the barber Mullen lost his nerve a bit and would swish the scissors behind the customer's neck with the menace of a metal hawk.

"What do you think of Tom coming out then? Who'd have thought it? There aren't many of us left, Old. The world full of wimps and all the girls, Old, all of them waiting for a real bloke, a bloke like you and me, Old, with a pair of balls, to come along and pin them against the wall, with a prick that holds, Old, no wind, that's what a girl wants, Old, for you to stick it in and leave her feeling meek and full, in her place, Old, that's what a girl wants."

Click, click. The scissors' killer beak.

So he decided not to get involved and head straight for The Glimmer Man instead. But he already felt stuck in the footsteps he had left on Arbour Hill, as if shackled by the wind. And he looked behind and came across that skinny, big-eared dog, painted black and white. He stopped, and the dog did the same. The ears, sure enough, were long and hung like a scarf. He walked on a bit, and the dog followed suit. Old M. came to a halt again, and the dog copied him. He did not know the animal, but the feeling did not seem to be mutual. When he called to it – in as impersonal a manner as might be, "Here, boy, come!" – he stroked the back of its neck. The skin was rough like a scouring pad and seemed as unfeeling as a pathologist's sheet. To show it some affection, he'd have had to give it a gentle kick in the muzzle. And that's exactly what he did.

The sign of The Glimmer Man soon took up his attention. He forgot the dog and crossed the road, dodging the lights.

At that time, he was still the only one at the bar. Maggie's blouse revealed the lingerie of her breasts. He loved that first pint of beer, when the pub was as clear of smoke as his head and the ballads seemed to issue from a water-tap.

"It's windy out, eh, Old?" said Maggie, folding her arms just where he would have done had he been able.

"That's right, it is." And he added in a tone that even he found mysterious,

"Though leaves are many, the root is one."

Maggie looked at him as if he had solved an enigma. She had not expected this of Old M., stuck as he always was in his own shadow, so to speak. These things are paid with a smile. So she leaned over the bar, not without first glancing sideways to see if anyone was looking, and brought her face near, fixing him with her mischievous eyes, in the way of a woman who is going to stoke the warm peat-fire.

"In the lying days of my youth I swayed my flowers in the sun," Maggie sweetly soughed.

Old M. felt the flames rise up from the cauldron of his insides. All the years of monosyllables burned now, piled up like fallen leaves. The moment at which the beer passes from one hand to another, the ephemeral bond of a note or coin, was all that linked him to this woman. Many years on the other side of the bar, watching, day by day, the change in her hair, her cleavage, the colour of her nails. Every night he placed a ring in those hands, when he went to pay.

And now the weights of the wall clock in The Glimmer Man turned the Universe.

Maggie calmly moved away, as if drawn by the same gravity that had taken so many years to attract her to his side. The ivy of the music entwined about the scrolls of distant looks. Had Old M. found the word, he'd have used nostalgia to describe the smoke from the Benson & Hedges that he brought to his lips. As if that gesture from Maggie belonged to a fairy or a hurricane, everything had taken on a new meaning, which also embraced what had happened to him in the past. As it advanced, the clock revealed an ancient furrow, in which all the disorders sprouted. The fact of being born, for example, was something that had made him feel ashamed until today, an excessive occurrence. He never grew anxious – that would have been exaggerated, an added problem, as well – but he tried to avoid the things that had caused him most shame.

Once he had a fall in front of the fruit market on St Michan's Street. The pavement was icy and Old M. slipped up on his back.

Potatoes rolled out of the bag and along the street like billiard-balls directed by the Devil. He avoided that place for ever after. This, to him, was the hurt of shame, similar to the hurt received when you fall on your sacrum. The world is a stage where people are looking out to see who lands on their backside.

"Touch them, Old," the woman selling tomatoes on Moore Street had said to him.

And when he did, she shouted at the top of her voice, "They're not pricks, Old. However much you touch them, they won't get hard."

But today, on leaving The Glimmer Man, Old M. was a different person. He wasn't even bothered when Mr Morgan asked him whether the dog following him was his.

"No, it's not mine, Mr Morgan."

"He looks like he hasn't eaten since the Year of the Plague. You should feed him better, Old M."

"The truth is, Mr Morgan, that it's not mine."

And the deaf old fool keeps on going.

"The fleas will eat him up. Your father wouldn't like to see him in such a state."

Old M. looked at the dog and the dog looked at him. Any other time and he'd have done his utmost to explain himself. But, strangely, his sacrum did not hurt. A gust of wind came to his aid.

"You know, Mr Morgan, though leaves are many, the root is one."

The elderly man, pensive, and seemingly intimidated by something invisible, paid attention for the first time.

"That's right, boy, that's right," he said before disappearing down the funnel of night.

"You're skinny and you're ugly," said Old M. to the dog, when they were alone. "Jesus, how skinny and ugly and sad you are! Listen, Big Ears. Old is going to Kavanagh's now for another drink and you're going back the way you came, OK? Go on then, shoo!"

He felt strange giving orders. He'd never had anyone to give them to and besides, he thought, it was better to receive them. The entire shame in an order belongs to the person responsible for it. He saw himself on the parade-ground, during military training, holding on to a mule. There was a sergeant there who shouted, "Earthquake!" – the animal's name – and he, Old, would take a step forward, stand to attention and reply, "Present!"

He felt a shooting pain, like a pin-prick, in his sacrum.

"Go on, off you go," he said to the dog. He hunched his shoulders and entered Kavanagh's.

"Listen, Old," said Bruton, "everything you hear about pig-meat is a porky-pie. Did you know that pork is the best for your cholesterol? I bet you didn't know that, did you, Old?"

Bruton, John Bruton, was wearing a tie today and loosened the knot every time he took a long drink. As far as he knew, Bruton had no financial interest in the pig industry, and so his enthusiasm was worthy of the greatest consideration.

"The truth, Mr Bruton, is that states of opinion are not always founded on what we might call a reasonable basis."

John Bruton repositioned his tie and looked at Old M. with a spark of curiosity. He had started talking to him, in the first place, because he could not keep quiet. And secondly, because there was no one else to hand at the bar of Kavanagh's at that time.

"That's right, Old. I like what you've said. My point exactly. People simply pass on what they've heard others say. So-and-so told me. Yes, but who told you? Oh, I don't know! Well, let's see! Why is pork bad for your cholesterol? I don't know, that's just what I've heard. Yes, but by whom, when and where was it verified scientifically. Scientiiiiifically. That is the question."

"Yes, Mr Bruton. It's all relative. General Grant, for example, who conquered the Southerners in the United States, would drink a bottle every night. Or more. So some went and complained to

President Lincoln, accusing Grant of being a drunk. So Lincoln goes and says to them, 'Gentlemen, I should like to know what it is that Grant drinks, to send a few bottles of the same to all the other generals.'"

Bruton was struck with surprise, as if in the process of unravelling the story. Then he burst out laughing and slapped Old M. on the back.

"Excellent, Old! Excellent story! Where did you get it? It's very good!"

"I must have read it somewhere, I don't know, I just remembered . . ."

The idea of Old M. with something in his hands to read seemed to increase Bruton's surprise. The image that he had of him was of a grey, dim-witted man, incapable of stringing together a sentence with style.

"It's good to read, Old. Shame that . . . It's an excellent story! I should like to know what Grant drinks to send a few bottles to the other generals. Brilliant, Old!"

He finished his pint of beer, in high spirits as a result of the story, and called to the barman. "Let's have another one, Old! On the house!"

"Thank you, Mr Bruton, that's very kind. But I have to go."

It was the first time he had been offered a drink without there being a special favour involved. In other circumstances, he would have accepted immediately. He would have been embarrassed to say no, to think that Mr Bruton might feel offended. He did not know why he had decided to go, but he thought that it was right and decided to do so.

"One more for the road, Old. It's windy out."

A band of dry birds and dead butterflies fluttered about inside his head, saying, "Though leaves are many, the root is one." But he kept silent. Mr Bruton would have latched on to the sentence and prolonged the evening. Perhaps, if he'd not found a suitable link, he'd have felt humiliated.

"I appreciate it, Mr Bruton. And if you don't mind, I'll have that pint another day with great pleasure."

"Of course, Old. Whenever you like."

"*Slán agat*, Mr Bruton."

"*Slán abhaile*, Old."

The dog was waiting at the door and Old M. did his best to frighten it off. It didn't even growl back. On the contrary, it allowed itself to be led. They descended Manor Street and took a short cut opposite Stanhope Street School along the Victorian terraces. The streetlamps projected two shadows coupled in a single being with six feet and very long ears. Old M. laughed. It was the first time he had laughed at himself and he felt happy. The comical shadow turned to him and said,

"Now I may wither into the truth."

Back at Temple Villas, he opened the gate and let the dog through, "You're right, Pa, Mrs O'Leary's rosebushes even look lovely at night."

Behind them, like a band of sparrows startled by Autumn's broom, came all the dry leaves.